Night Birds

a novel by

Lisa Snellings and Alan M. Clark

IFD Publishing

P.O. Box 40776, Eugene, Oregon 97404, U.S.A.
www.ifdpublishing.com

Night Birds

ISBN: 979-8-9852827-3-3
Printed in the United States of America

Acknowlegdments

Thanks to Aubrey Snellings, Orion Clark, Pete Clark, Roland and Robert Chisolm, Shield Bonnichsen, Dani Dowler, Cobalt, Jan Thie, Carla Emmons, Kristi Stowe, James Bolan, Bev Melven, Syd Mooney, Jill Freeman, Elise Matthesen, Jackie Pearce, Sally Jennings, Vernon Miller, Sigmund Hsu, Melody Kees Clark, Jill Bauman, and Cynthia Drewek.

Night Birds

a novel by

Lisa Snellings and Alan M. Clark

Publishing

Eugene, Oregon

The Blimp
1963

Daddy called me Rooster, since most mornings he found me awake when he arose. I was a bird, but not that one. No, I was a night owl, up most of the dark hours watching and listening in the quiet.

I didn't start out that way. I'd begun in life sleeping soundly.

What troubled my sleep started with the steam whistle at the cotton mill where my father worked. Normally it blew at shift changes, 8AM and 4PM. If the whistle sounded any other time, folks sat up and took notice, because that meant something terrible had happened.

The mill had a long history of terrible things happening. The worst stories that went around town had always been about accidents at the mill. Of course they grew more dreadful still as the tales passed from one child to another on the playground, around campfires, and under the bleachers at little league games.

The first time I truly noticed the whistle, I was five and knew nothing of these legends. The moment the sound startled me, a big shadow crept over my back yard and I looked up. A blimp, I would later learn, but in that moment the shadow belonged to a silver monster in the sky, and the whistle had been its scream. As the thing drew closer, I heard an ominous droning. I scrambled for cover under my porch. The drone got louder, then changed pitch, moving off into the distance.

I saw movement in the corner of my eye, something pale among the short brick columns supporting the house. A girl, about my size. She wore a pink sack, more like a nightgown than a dress. What was she doing under my house? Maybe she was playing, and I could join in. She stared at me with big, dark eyes in the palest face I'd ever seen.

"Little girl," I called out, and made my way on hands and knees between the columns through the sand, sticks, and leaves that had been blown under the house. My knee pressed down on something sharp and I stopped to look.

A toy car, one of my brother's, I guessed.

When I looked back up, I could not see the girl. Searching for her, I crawled forward, calling out "Hello? Little girl?"

I heard my parents' muffled voices and crawled to a spot directly under the kitchen where, once before, I'd listened to a conversation between Mama and Ruth, the woman hired to help around the house.

"I hate that sound," I heard Mama say sharply. "I nearly jump out of my skin every time it blows."

I thought she meant the silver monster's scream, and wondered if she'd become frightened like I had.

"Hate it all you want," Daddy said, "but I'm the one who has to go down there. Whatever has happened is not going to be pretty."

His footsteps crossed the floor to the door, then the back porch, and crunched into the drive as he hurried to his car. He wasn't afraid! Maybe he would go scare the monster away. Dust from his hasty departure blew under the house, choking me. I had to get out of there.

I'd forgotten all about the strange girl.

Inside the house, I found Mama staring out the kitchen window. She had a troubled look, standing with her hands tightly gripping her elbows.

"What's wrong, Mama?"

She started, rubbed her hands hard against her apron.

"Is Daddy gonna be okay?"

"Yes, he'll take care of it." she said, her voice sounding far away. "Go wash your hands for lunch."

Just to see her in such a swivet, I knew I should be troubled, but I also knew Daddy would fix everything. He always did.

Standing at the bathroom sink, I rolled the soap in my hands and thought about the little girl under the house. Though she sure looked strange, I'd be looking for her to play with first chance.

When Daddy came home and we sat for dinner, I asked him about the screaming sky monster.

"Is that a cartoon?" he asked.

"No, It's in the sky."

"Oh, an airplane," he said.

Mama laughed, said, "You have quite an imagination," and kissed me on the head.

Mama had smiled at me, so I knew she wasn't afraid anymore.

All seemed right with the world again.

~ ~ ~

Some weeks later, at Mrs. Eunice Cleary's house, I sat in the waiting room while she finished giving a piano lesson to the student ahead of me. I winced at each sour note while thumbing through a comic book that became more frightening with each new page. I'd picked it because I knew the Archie ones by heart, and had found all the hidden objects in the one copy of Highlights. Turning the page, I discovered a picture of a woman on a bed, her mouth wide in a terrified scream, as snakes slithered out from between her legs. I wadded the comic book up and shoved it under the couch cushion. Wiping my hands on my shorts, I did my best to forget what I'd seen. Somehow I knew I wasn't meant to see that, and had to wonder how it had gotten there. I didn't look at the student leaving, embarrassed at the thought that he might know what I'd seen.

My turn to enter the music room. Mrs. Cleary sat in her chair the same as always, but she hunched oddly, as if shrinking into its cushions. Red rimmed her eyes. The room smelled sweetly of oranges. She set down the orange she'd been peeling when I entered and wiped her hands on a napkin alongside a bowl of peels. Another bowl held several oranges. Someone had eaten a lot of the fruit. Mrs. Eunice blew her runny nose into her napkin.

"Would you like one, dear?" she asked.

"No ma'am," I said, "I'll get sticky on your piano."

"Of course," she said, "what *am* I thinking?" She bent over and wept, her shoulders shaking.

I stood there not knowing what to do. Had I done something wrong? Should I have taken the orange?

She mopped at her face, sat upright with a weak smile, and patted the piano bench. "Sit down, child. Despite our heartaches, we must all carry on."

What heartache did we suffer? I wondered. Then the thought occurred that she meant strictly her own heartache.

"Please open your book to the new lesson."

I thumbed past the pages with gummed, gold stars on them to the new piece I'd been practicing at home.

Before I'd played a single note, the cuckoo clock's bird called four times from out in the waiting room, followed by the scream of the silver sky monster.

Mrs. Cleary cried out, buried her face in her napkin, and started weeping again.

I looked toward the window. Though I'd heard its scream a few times, I hadn't seen the monster or its shadow since the day I hid under the house and saw the pale girl. Hidden indoors, I felt much safer.

"Dear child," she said. "I-I'm so sorry, but I must go lie down."

I took her sticky hands in mine and looked her in the eye. "It's all right," I said, trying to calm her. "It won't come after us. It'll just fly on by."

She stared at me for a moment as if I wasn't there, then took her hands back, sniffed, and said, "You may sit in the waiting room until your father arrives." She hurried from the room.

Left with just imagination to answer my questions, I had to wonder if the monster had come after her before, maybe chased her. I looked around the room, saw the oranges and peels, Mrs. Cleary's discarded napkin. She'd left the door to the rest of the house open. She never allowed that. What was going on? Maybe she'd eaten too many oranges. I ate too many plums once and pooped my pants. Maybe something like that had happened and she was embarrassed.

Remembering the horrible comic, I decided I'd rather wait for Daddy on the doorstep. Outside, to my surprise, I found him leaning against our car in the drive. Seeing me, he looked at his watch, dropped his cigarette, and snuffed it out with his foot.

"Ready to go early, huh, Rooster?"

"She heard the monster and got all upset."

He frowned, turned his eyes to Mrs. Cleary's door and back to me. "I see."

He opened the car door. I gave him my lesson book, slid across the seat to my side, and we started for home; away from the horrible comic, the smell of oranges, and Mrs. Cleary's mysterious heartache. Unsettled, I huddled into myself, my knees drawn up to my chest, my hands bunched up under my chin. I would have liked to hug Daddy, but I couldn't while he drove the car. My summer clothes felt too thin, the sun too bright.

I felt Daddy looking at me. He reached over, opened the glove box, and pulled out my Bunny, the stuffed one I'd had since before I could remember. I grabbed the toy and held it tight against me, resting my chin between its ears.

"You'll have to forgive your piano teacher," Daddy said, glancing at me with an earnest look, "She lost her husband a few weeks ago."

"Lost him? Did the monster in the sky get him?"

He gave me a funny look, then shook his head, "No, Rooster, he was in an accident at the mill."

"Will he be found?"

"No, honey, it's not the same kind of lost. He's passed away, gone to heaven."

"That's forever, right?"

"Yes, and that's why she's so sad."

Not understanding, I grew quiet and nuzzled bunny tighter. The familiar smell of the stuffed animal rose up and helped ease my mind.

Daddy glanced at me once, twice, and said, "all living creatures pass away sometime."

"To heaven?"

"Well, not quite all."

He meant that animals would not go to heaven. We'd had a conversation about that once before, one I didn't like.

Thinking about how Bunny would never leave me to go to heaven or anywhere else gave me comfort. Because the stuffed animal wasn't exactly alive, it would never die.

But I could lose Bunny, accidentally leave it somewhere. Imagining Bunny lost and alone someplace dark and dreary brought back all my unease.

The little lost girl under the house sprang to mind. Had she been misplaced?

And how did I know she was lost?

The Man in the Black Fedora
1965

I rode in the back seat of Mama's car on our way home from the grocery store in the early evening of a November day. A light drizzle had started just as the streetlights stuttered on. The sour mood I'd had that morning in school improved about noon when we'd learned that snow had been predicted for that night. The kids at school had been worked up about the possibility all afternoon, looking out the windows instead of at the blackboard. Miss Yonce didn't care; she seemed as excited as the students.

Too small to easily see the road ahead through the windshield, I tried sitting up and peering around the beehive Mama had paid some lady to torture her hair into—every lovely, auburn strand lacquered into place. Before bed, she would wrap the "do" in toilet paper. My scalp itched just thinking about it.

Normally, my grandmother would be with us, and I'd be chewing contentedly on the Rolaids she offered in place of mints. They tasted of the inside of her purse, something of leather and brass maybe. But she hadn't come this time, and the empty seat gave me a little pang in my stomach, because Mama and Grandma didn't really get along all that well. I had to wonder, if I didn't ask for it, would Grandma ever go anywhere with us.

Mama had explained Grandma's absence before we left home. I hadn't paid much attention to what I thought to be an excuse as I rushed around, changing from school clothes into pants while trying not to pull the Band-Aid off my knee. The one before had gone astray and got twisted up in my sock.

"Hurry up," Mama said. "We must get back before the weather sets in."

She always expected the worst.

We didn't get much snow in that part of South Carolina. When we did, it really came down.

Grandma probably had some appointment—maybe some farmer with warts or something. She was a healer, part-time, of the "talking" variety. She used words—many I didn't understand—and home-made remedies to take away the pain of burns, heal other aches, even to soothe a broken heart. If she kept it on the quiet and got paid mostly in eggs or odd jobs, the church turned a blind eye to her practical medicine and she kept a steady trickle of grateful, trusting clients. She didn't usually see them on market day.

I must've been about seven and I didn't have eyeglasses yet. If I'd had them, I might not have seen what I saw. Some things are better seen without the details, which mostly just show on the fragile outsides. Details can be a distraction, like red lipstick to cover up disappointment. I couldn't count the many times Mama had looked at me with a troubled expression, only to turn away and hastily apply her lipstick when she saw I'd noticed. Somehow, I stood in her way. Afraid I wouldn't like the answer, I didn't ask about it.

The rain came down harder and the drops got smaller. I willed snow to fall, looking hopefully for flakes revealed in the headlights. Mama had bought a bag of hard candies from a Christmas display in the produce section of the grocery store. I'd wanted the big, soft peppermints. She had argued that those would get sticky in damp weather. Mesmerized by the wipers' regular rhythm, I rolled a fat butterscotch disk around my tongue. Still on the highway, we hadn't yet turned off onto the long forest-lined route home, Pine Log Road. So I settled into my seat and let my mind wander to snowball fights, snowmen, and sledding.

The wipers, which had flicked back and forth steadily, seemed to pause, just as Mama gasped and hit the brakes hard. The momentum pulled me violently from my seat, but the lap belt caught me. The oily smell of tires scrubbed hot against wet pavement grew sharp and distinct. The whole world flew by sideways and in slow-motion. The stretched moment ended abruptly. All that had been gluey, weightless, and dreamlike came down hard, including me. I slammed back against my seat.

The next thing I knew, my door opened with a rush of cold air and Mama's face pressed close. I saw her mouth working. Her voice sounded disconnected and distant.

"Answer me! *Answer me!*"

I tried. No sound came out. The candy had lodged in my throat. I couldn't take a breath. Panic had me clawing at my neck. Mama saw, unhooked the belt, and jerked me up by my arms like a ragdoll. I followed a deafening roar down to blackness.

~ ~ ~

That morning, after he'd showered, shaved and dressed, I'd followed Daddy as he got ready for work. In the bedroom, he scooped off the dresser all that belonged in his pockets and started sorting; cigarettes and matchbook in his shirt pocket, wallet in his left-rear pants pocket, keys in his right-front, folding knife and pocket change in the left-front. I'd become fascinated to find that Daddy always placed his stuff in the same pockets. Why would he do that?

He paused to show me his flattened lucky coin. "Still got your penny, Rooster?"

I pulled mine out and showed him. He gave me his smile, his warm eyes loving. I remembered the day we put them on the railroad tracks and waited for the train to come along and flatten them. We'd been fishing in the river below the train trestle and had taken a break to climb up to the tracks. We sat on the rails that had warmed in the sun, ate crackers with canned sausages, and shared a bottle of soda before returning to our fishing. I forgot all about our pennies until the four-thirty train went across the trestle and Daddy said, "let's go see what they look like." We'd found them flattened into thin oblong shapes, the images in relief on the coins elongated and harder to make out.

Helen, my older sister, paused in the doorway, adjusting her candy striper uniform. "You know, *you* were almost a Penny."

"But I'm a girl," I told her, as she moved on to the kitchen.

"No," Daddy said, "she means we almost named you that. Your mother lost a baby that would have been your older sister, between you and Will. We planned to name *her* Penny. When you came along later, I wanted to call you Penny, but your mother said you should have your own name."

I remembered he'd used the word *lost* when talking about Mr. Cleary's death, and that had led me to thinking about the girl I'd seen under the house. Not knowing what to call her, I decided right then to give her the name Penny. That seemed like a nice name.

Daddy left for the mill and I joined Helen at the kitchen table. She had toast with marmalade—yuck! I had a bowl of cornflakes and milk.

"I was really looking forward to having a sister named Penny, even though she'd only be a half sister, like you."

"I'm not a half *anything*."

"It just means we had different fathers, that's all." She took a sip of her coffee. Again, yuck, and black too! "Will and I had a different father from you."

"You call Daddy, *Daddy*."

"I call him that because I love him. Our father died when Will was so young, he probably doesn't remember him much."

14

"Did Mama love your daddy too?"

"Of course, she did."

"Who will she be married to in Heaven?"

Helen set her cup down, gazed at the ceiling, looking troubled, "That's a good question. I've never really thought about that."

As I was about to ask something else really important, a beeping horn out front interrupted. "Jackie's here," Helen said. "Got to go." She left her dirty dishes on the table, picked up her purse, and hurried out in her crisp, red and white-striped uniform.

I was left wondering: *If Mama can only have one husband in heaven, will I still be Daddy's Rooster?*

~ ~ ~

This must be what time travel feels like. Or dying. Or being born. Something always gets lost in the transactions.

My coat lay on the ground, lit by blurry lights from another car. The fabric darkened as water soaked in. Someone held me while I pulled in cold air. A man. I felt his strength and saw his shoes—black wingtips, smooth, and especially shiny—with delicate stitching and drops arranged on them like little glass beads.

He stopped pounding my back, and with a "There, now" he lifted me to my feet and into my mother's embrace. She would've been about thirty-eight at the time. Her rouge had all washed away, and her hair hung in wet, sticky ringlets—some with bobby pins clinging on them like tinsel, catching the light.

Mama looked raw, and frightened, and…beautiful. Most of all, she looked relieved. I did not stand in her way in that moment.

I buried my face in the damp, earthy wool of her skirt. The rain had soaked through the cuffs of her blouse so that the little holly designs looked painted onto her wrists.

"It was right in front of me—I *must* have hit it!"

Her voice sounded so foreign. The voice of someone who existed without me. I felt particularly small, looking up at the two of them. She gazed into the face of a man wearing a black hat, a fedora. My daddy had one of those too, a dark gray one for church. The stranger had a handsome face, a squared jaw, and the tiniest bit of whisker stubble, his good looks enhanced by an earnest frown of concern. Somehow, I could see that Mama found him handsome too, and for the first time, I saw her as her own person, not just Daddy's wife and my mother.

"I'm sure you're right," he said. "But there's no sign of a deer, and no damage to your grill, just the tire marks."

My legs began to tremble. I wanted Daddy. I wanted to be home in my bed, dry and warm, and *yesterday*.

"Oh honey." Mama said, pulling me in closer. She wiped at her eyes with the man's handkerchief, then looked skyward with a nervous laugh. Rain pelted her cheeks.

"Will you be able to drive?" the man asked. He bent to retrieve our coats from the pavement. Mama's arm tightened around my shoulders as she held the folded white rectangle out in her other hand.

We don't have much farther to go. I'm so glad you happened to be here. I must've looked like a crazy person! You saved my girl!"

"Of course. She'll be achy, but she'll sleep well tonight." He chuckled.

He patted the back of her hand and took the handkerchief. Her eyes lingered on him even as he turned away to squat down at my eye level.

"And you, be careful with candy, young lady, especially butterscotch. It's the devil's favorite." His eyes twinkled.

And that's when I saw. The smile was false, bleak, without emotion. The eyes, though blue like mine, held vast distances. I couldn't look away. Much as I wanted to pull back, I had a sudden, puzzling need for his approval. The feeling was one I would only understand years later while studying animals and learning more of the vocabulary of fear. The single word I have to describe my reaction is *Primal.*

Much worse than that, he winked at me. The wink said he knew that I'd seen past his surface details. The wink told me he wanted me to know he knew. I felt like he knew me and where I lived. I wanted to get away from him.

He stood and tucked the handkerchief that had soaked up my mother's tears in his pocket. Then he adjusted his hat, turned, and walked away, like any man in fine shoes, which he most certainly was not.

At home, I sat in the bathtub, clutching a mug of warm milk. Indeed, I had grown achy, with bruises on both my skinny hip bones, a stiff neck, and a sore throat. Mama had given me four aspirin to chew up. Moments later, she gave me two more. They were chalky and tasted vaguely like orange. She'd wrapped her hair in a towel. I saw a bruise on her cheek. As she bent to kiss my head, I'd kept my eyes on the milk. I'd already seen and been seen too much that day.

While soaking, I watched Mama and Daddy through the bathroom doorway. They sat in the kitchen drinking coffee and talking. Mama described what happened to us, and kept insisting she'd seen something in the headlights.

"Lucy said she thought you might know the fellow who stopped to help," Daddy said.

"Oh, *no!*" Mama said, "He was a stranger. And I mean *strange!* There was something about him that didn't sit right with me."

That wasn't what *I* recalled. She had seemed quite taken with him.

I *did* remember not liking the way he touched her when he took the handkerchief back. Though she'd seemed comfortable with him, I didn't want him to have Mama's tears in his pocket.

"Do you remember me telling you about the guy that showed up at the mill," Daddy asked, "the one trying to sell me his car?"

"Yes, so and so's cousin?"

"Uh huh, that's the one, Todd Dobbs. Anyway, the deal was too good to be true. Something about the guy—I just knew he was a swindler."

"You think the guy that helped us was a *criminal* of some sort?" She'd whispered the words with too much drama.

Daddy glanced toward me like he did when he wanted to make sure I wasn't listening. We smiled at each other.

He turned back to Mama and nodded.

"Well," she said, shaking her head. "*Something* ran in front of the car. That was the *real* danger."

"I'll take another look at the front bumper and fenders in tomorrow's light," he said, and added a little more brandy to her coffee.

A cut glass dish of the holiday candy sat on the table between them, all shine and hard edges. Looking at it, I stroked my throat. Our coats swung almost imperceptibly in the warm air from the furnace. The kitchen faucet dripped.

Telling the tale, Mama had left out so much. In the future, I would too. I wanted to stuff all of it into some deep, forgotten place until springtime. Spring was ages away. By then, Mama would have decided she'd hit the brakes for a trick of the light.

But for now, I'd want to be careful with my words and my thoughts. Otherwise, Grandma would sniff me out and ask questions. Annie Maude didn't miss much. My own questions nagged at me. What would've happened if she'd been there in the car? Did this thing happen because she wasn't? I didn't want to think the man in the black fedora could be any place near her. I didn't want to believe in a God who could let the two of them become acquainted, her and the man in the black fedora. That would be a world that didn't make any sense. I'd keep my mouth shut. And most especially, I wouldn't tell anyone, ever, that I too saw the *something* zip through the headlights. That was no deer.

I put the mug of milk on the floor and slid down to rest my head on the tub's edge. The water, up to my chin, felt warm and comforting, a vast, welcoming ocean with islands of Mr. Bubble around my knees. On one of them, the Band-Aid floated.

Outside, through the small bathroom window, the rain had turned into snow. Big, puffy flakes came down in the porch light. I closed my eyes.

Most probably, there would be no school the next day.

And most certainly, I would not sleep well that night.

Two Pennies
1966

Over time, I caught glimpses of the little pale girl I'd named Penny, sometimes in the house at night. And with time, I decided she must be a ghost. While that frightened me, I remained fascinated with the idea of playing with her. I even chased her one night all through the house, careful not to awaken my family. I didn't catch her. The first time she spoke to me, the first time I touched her, was in the evening after one of the worst days ever.

That morning, I'd argued with Mama over the dress I would wear to school. She'd won, of course. I hated that dress. The black and red plaid pattern, the long sleeves and deep pockets were nice enough, but it also had an enormous, bright white collar that draped over my bony shoulders like two ill-assigned wings. She'd made the dress herself, with skill and care, which accounts for why she rescued it once again from the nethers of my closet, where I'd hoped the garment would be forgotten. Now the thing hung on the back of my door, starched up and ready to ruin another day. On that gray and overcast Friday in October, I saw my doom.

I retaliated by not eating a bite of breakfast. I paused at the sight of my toothbrush, then turned a rebellious shoulder and went to the hall to wriggle into my coat. Yanking my hat on low, I stomped out through the back door and down the steps without a word—kept stomping until I got out of sight of the house. Though full of my own piss and vinegar, I walked more reasonably the rest of the way to school. Once in the classroom, I tried to keep my coat on, complaining of the cold.

"It's warm enough in here," Miss Yonce said, looking over the top of her glasses at me.

I lingered in the cloakroom, wishing I could stay there with the dust motes in the morning light. As she started the roll call, I allowed myself a long sigh, put my coat on a hook, and walked to my desk.

I'd about made it there too, when Eddy Greenwood snickered and Tommy Milliner said, "Lookit the little angel!" Tommy lived on Laurel Drive, in the good part of town, and seemed to think it his duty to remind me that I did not. He usually made cutting statements meant to single me out as coming from a poor family.

By the time I sat in my seat, the hot shame had reached my temples. I could see the white of the collar from the corners of my eyes, even though I tried not to. My fingers found the flattened penny I carried in my pocket, and turned it over and over. I'd always thought of the oblong coin as having had the power of an entire locomotive pounded into it. On that day, I figured I might need to borrow some of that.

Chet Boyd, my only real friend in third grade, gave me a sidelong look of sympathy. He lived several doors down from me. His house, even in summer, had the musty smell of burning leaves. His mother, Mrs. Boyd, while never quite delighted to see me, wasn't unkind. In fact, she occasionally gave me one of the glass animals she collected. I often imagined myself there among her miniature menagerie and just as small.

Soon as Miss Yonce stood and spoke, I obediently turned to the page she specified and the lesson began.

~ ~ ~

With the tall windows in the lunchroom completely fogged up, hiding the ordinary maintenance building and the wall of shrubs that stood not far away, I could decide it was all a mystery and then anything could be out there.

We had meatloaf that day, with pungent mustard greens and enormous biscuits baked right there in the kitchen. The bread scents still hung in the warm air. The clatter of trays and silverware played over a constant murmur of voices. We each had a serving of canned grapefruit in the corner squares of our trays. I sat between Mark and Connie, who were discussing Mark's dare; to eat some grapefruit and chase it with a swallow of milk. The dread combo could make you puke, according to Mark's fifth-grade brother. Mark downed several of the bitter wedges and paused dramatically, milk carton to lips. His gleeful eyes watched the others as they leaned in eagerly.

Not me. I knew something that tasted a whole lot worse. My fingers found the hard contour of my lucky penny through the wool of my dress.

Ravenous after skipping breakfast, I ignored the idiots and took a big mouthful of my biscuit. So big, in fact, I needed to wash it down and raised my milk to take a drink.

"Blaaahh!" Mark cried out, spitting, sputtering, and flailing. His elbow bumped mine. Before I could blink, my own carton tumbled into my lap. Milk went everywhere.

Laughter rang out, drawing all eyes to our table. Miss Yonce hurried over.

Mark would spend some time at the blackboard back in the classroom, with his nose in a chalk circle reserved for such clowns. The big clock above the lunchroom door read eleven thirty. The day was shaping up to be a long one. I followed Miss Yonce out of the room, the hated dress clinging to my legs, cold and wet. I still had a mouthful of biscuit. I swallowed it down dry, began to choke, and panicked, remembering the butterscotch. Eyes watering, I finally got the thick dough down and took a grateful breath, glad I didn't have to draw more attention to myself.

Ahead of me, Miss Yonce's shoes clomped along the corridor, past the alcohol smell of the nurse's station to the Lost and Found, where boxes of donated clothes stood by for such emergencies.

My hope rose as she reached into a box, and died as she came up with a blue monstrosity of butterflies and wrinkles and shook the dress out. Miss Yonce let out a delicate sneeze at the stirred-up dust. She gave me a look that said she'd hear no arguments.

I lifted my arms. She removed my wet dress and deftly worked the even-worse one over my head. My hair crackled with static from the stiff fabric.

A prisoner resigned to her fate, I silently followed her back to the classroom.

"Put a penny in your mouth—that'll stop your blubbering," my tormentor of a brother, Will, had told me. That turned out to be true, the shocking taste worked like a charm. That was the real reason I kept the coin with me.

Already I lived in a mill house, was skinny, and had an overbite. I couldn't afford to be a crybaby too.

Once settled back at my desk, I glanced around to make sure no one watched me, then put a fingertip to my tongue. That would have to do, since my penny remained in the pocket of the wet dress, which lay, rolled up in a paper bag, beneath my desk. I shuddered at the bitter, copper taste. That had to be worse than grapefruit and milk.

No more comments came from Edward or Tommy. Nobody even looked my way, including Chet. That was somehow worse than teasing. I felt the sting of fresh tears, so I put two coppery fingers in my mouth and stared hard at Mark's back, noting how his shoulders slumped as he stood in his own shame at the blackboard.

Miss Yonce surveyed the classroom, her face a mask of warning against further shenanigans. "We'll work on math for the rest of the day," she announced.

Good. I was confident with numbers. No judgement in arithmetic, only rules and facts that were fair and made sense. I opened my notebook and had started to tackle the first problem when my pencil lead broke. My heart sank. I slid out of my seat and moved reluctantly toward the sharpener, which waited in mocking silence, bolted onto the front wall beside the blackboard. As I passed Edward's desk, a snicker escaped him—he couldn't help himself. I know that now. Years later, following Daddy's death, Edward—plump, balding, and with a kind face—wrangled a laugh out of me at the funeral. Yet on that Friday, in Miss Yonce's third grade classroom, he was just the other clown who ended up with his nose in a chalk circle.

Before setting out for home after school, I checked the bag and both pockets of the dress, but didn't find my penny. The day had been bad enough. Losing the penny made things worse. My hope was to search through the Lost and Found the next day. I stuffed the bag under my arm and walked home in the cloudy afternoon, glad to be back in my coat. The maintenance building and wall of shrubs stood square and plain. The pines swayed in the breeze, taking no notice of me.

That evening following dinner—meatloaf—I sat with Bunny in the chair by the grandfather clock in the hall. I whispered in the stuffed rabbit's ear, complaining about my crappy day; an unsatisfying, one-sided conversation.

That spot in the hall, out of sight from the living room, had always been a good one for eavesdropping on my parents. They had been in there, talking in serious tones since dinner ended, and hadn't noticed the late hour, well past my bedtime. If I wanted to know anything about anything, I had to steal the information. So there I sat, as I often did, in my own little corner of crime.

They became quiet. I got up and crept toward the doorway to see what they were up to. By the time I got there, I recognized the first notes of Floyd Cramer's soulful waltz, "Last Date." Mama and Daddy sat hip to hip on the piano bench, each playing a part of the melody to make the song whole. Mama missed a key and hit a sour note. She giggled and leaned into Daddy. He kissed her forehead and they continued the piece without missing a beat.

I realized I'd witnessed true love. Even with all the ups and downs of daily life, they had a real affection for each other. I'm not certain I'd ever seen that before.

Feeling like an intruder, I sat back down and told Bunny, "People get married for a reason, I guess."

I sensed Penny before I saw her. My skin crawled with a terrible prickling and I went cold with dread, despite all my past eagerness to see her. I squeezed my eyes shut, a thin hope against the truth of Penny. I *did* and I did *not* want her to appear. When I opened my eyes, she'd got way too close and I started, strangling a cry. I saw the black pools of her eyes and felt the electric charge of her hair. Her dark locks moved like she floated in water. I'd become paralyzed, unblinking. If I hadn't already peed, I would have right then.

So close, right at my ear, she whispered, "You're in my seat." She drifted back and pointed at Bunny. "And that's *not* yours."

She smelled of dust, and rain, and something else that reminded me of the big ice box on the back porch—a cold smell.

Though she held my attention like nothing else, I couldn't help wondering, *If Bunny isn't mine, then who does it belong to?*

Like she'd heard my thought, she said, "My bunny."

That was crazy, yet I had no answer for her. I clutched Bunny tighter.

Penny smiled knowingly, took my hand, and closed it inside both of hers, pale and cold as fish. "I'm sorry about the milk," she said, and gave my forehead a chilly kiss. A moment later, she vanished like smoke from a match.

I exhaled. My parents' muted conversation returned. When I opened my fingers, my train-flattened, lucky coin, minted in 1926, lay in my palm. The penny must've been in the bag—*must* have been.

My shaky legs carried me back up the stairs to my room. I put the penny on the mantel, fell onto my bed, and cried hard into my pillow, unable to banish the image of the little girl's black eyes from my head.

Exhausted, I lay for a while, breathing. If that was playing with Penny, I wasn't sure I wanted more. I'd heard of people being scared to death. My house was haunted, and I'd been scared—really scared. Now that she'd gone, though, I felt emptied out, and oddly peaceful.

I waited for sleep to take me to morning, letting my thoughts wander on ahead of me, but not too far. The next day, Saturday—we had no school. Cornflakes, bacon, and cartoons on TV. Those things were comfortingly predictable. I found myself looking forward to that normal.

I wondered if Tommy Milliner had ever seen a ghost. Nah, he hadn't. If he had, he wouldn't be such an asshole. I decided I was better than Tommy. I'd been kissed by a ghost and lived to tell the tale. He probably would've crapped his pants. I felt the corners of my mouth lift with the hint of a smile.

Under the Bed with Annie Maude
1967

Grandma's house had been my second home since before I could remember, and though I could walk right in through the back porch, I always knocked first and waited for a reply, the screen door's loud rattle within its frame somehow an appropriate fanfare announcing my arrival.

"Come in, dear." she called out.

I found Annie Maude in her kitchen, sitting at the table, backlit by the steamed up window. She cradled a large bowl made of some dark, heavy wood in her lap, and slowly stirred its thick contents with a wooden spoon. The inky, green liquid seemed to follow the spoon, round and round. She set the bowl on the table and opened her arms for a hug. I hurried to give her one.

Looking me over, she said, "Did you forget to bring Bunny?"

"Nah, I'm getting too old to carry a stuffed animal," I said.

The truth: Once Penny had said Bunny belonged to her, I'd had a hard time holding the toy without feeling creepy. I hoped that would go away with time because I'd been left feeling a little lost.

"I don't even know where Bunny came from," I said.

"A gift from your father when you were just a toddler."

"Did it ever belong to someone else?"

She looked at me for a moment without answering, her expression unreadable. "Now that's an interesting question, but I don't have an answer for you." She turned back to whatever she had going on in the bowl.

I dropped the subject, yet couldn't help thinking my grandmother had lied to me. She must have had a good reason to do that, I told myself.

"What are you making?" I asked.

"It's a preparation for The Honorable Whitney H. Clanton's gout," she said in a mock-haughty manner. "Now, you're to keep that in your secret-keepin' place."

I felt trustworthy, a good feeling.

"Scoot down to the potato bin, dear," Grandma said. "Find the red one that looks like a heart, and mind what you touch."

Already, we'd begun to play. At least, that's the way I chose to see following her queer instructions. Sort of like a game.

The cellar door's glass knob felt cold. I made my way down the creaky stairs. By the time my toe found the last tread, I'd already begun to note the things in the cellar that I wouldn't touch with a ten-foot pole, like the tall, locked cabinet that had glass doors so thick with dust, all I could see inside was the dull gleam from numerous white jars. I didn't dare wipe the glass for a better look, and not just for fear I'd get in trouble. Other items tempted me, though, like the fancy, little cabinet, red with gold trim, that sat in the corner. I caught myself creeping toward the thing. That had happened before. Once, I'd gotten close enough to touch the cabinet before turning away.

Annie Maude spooked me plenty, but I'd never been afraid of her. I trusted her and she made me feel safe. I'd stayed over at her house most weekends since I'd been very little. She'd always seemed more motherly to me than Mama.

Annie Maude had a lot of rules at her house—some usual ones, like wiping your feet before entering, no running, and such like—and some *very* unusual ones.

I can't remember how old I'd been when she gave her first rule: "Never dig in that garden bed." I might have been five or six. At the time, we'd stood in her back yard and she'd pointed toward the flower bed between the persimmon tree and the shed. She then gave me a child's trowel and pail so I could play gardener. Did she want to tempt me?

And then her first odd rule: "Never enter the rooms on the west side of the house." She'd gestured to show me what side she meant.

Of course, I soon ached to find out what she had hidden. Annie Maude could have locked the doors to those rooms—all the skeleton keys remained in their keyholes. So, another temptation, a test?

With some, I didn't see the need, but, again, I tried to think of them as the rules of a game we played, especially since some came and went. A rule about not ringing the bell that sat on a table on the back porch went in place in early summer each year, and got lifted as fall approached. She would let me know when.

I wouldn't question the rules for the longest time. Yet more and more lately, I'd asked about the ones that seemed to make no sense.

"Windows may only be opened in odd numbers," she'd said on a hot day while we were opening the house. "A window cannot be opened unless another one or a door is already open at least a crack."

Although something about that plan bothered me, at least a year passed before I figured out how to question the rule. "What if the whole house is shut up," I asked her.

"That doesn't happen. I keep an attic window open a crack in summer, in winter, a cellar one."

One gloomy Saturday, she'd pointed out a high-backed, cane-bottomed chair that sat alone in the hall looking very uncomfortable. "No one has ever sat in that chair," she said, "and don't you be the first."

At times, I thought of her as a witch, since the worst of the rumors about her ran in that vein. All the same, I chose not to decide whether she stood for good or bad or whether she actually performed magic. Somehow, I understood that her deeds were her own, and not to be questioned.

Something scratched against the narrow cellar window above the little red cabinet. The wind? I got that chicken-skin feeling. Lost in thoughts, I'd got close to the red cabinet again. I spun around quick, and hurried to the vegetable bins.

With little rummaging, I found a right good, heart-shaped red potato.

Already spooked, I took the stairs too fast. A loud bump against the same window startled me. I squealed and leapt over the last step. Peals of laughter came from outside the house.

"Jimmy's here," Grandma called. "Stop your running Lucy, and go greet your cousin."

I ran out onto the back porch and opened the door. "Jimmy, you turd," I said, and hit him. "You scared the *shit* out of me," I whispered.

"Looks more like your heart," he said pointing to the red potato I still held. "Jumped clean out of your chest, did it? Scare-a-boo got you! And that's twice in a row, now." He held up two fingers, and shoved them in my face— his way of rubbing it in. "One more and you'll owe me a comic."

We'd been playing the game, Scare-a-boo, our own invention, for a couple of years. The object was to startle your opponent. Get three in a row without having been startled yourself and you win a comic book of your choice from your opponent's collection.

I punched him on the shoulder hard enough to get a yelp. Gloating over his win, he didn't even bother to hit me back.

"Bring me the potato," Annie Maude called out, "then show him the room I made up."

Taking Jimmy's hand, I pulled him into the kitchen.

Annie Maude wiped her hands on her apron, turned to us. "There's my boy," she said. "Now, where's my hug?"

He put his arms out stiffly, and she took him in a hug that looked to swallow him whole. Jimmy rolled his eyes at me. I stifled a giggle.

Upstairs, I showed him the guest room. He moved to the window and started to open the sash.

"Grandma is funny about her windows—just warning you."

"Ok…" He opened it halfway.

"Lunch," Annie Maude shouted up the stairs.

In the kitchen, she'd set out sandwiches and lemonade on the table.

"There aren't enough chairs," Jimmy said. "I'll get the one in the hall."

I looked to Annie Maude, expecting her to say something. She put her hand on my shoulder. When I opened my mouth, she pressed down with her hand, and I knew she wanted me to stay quiet. Why?

Jimmy brought in the chair that had never been used, put it at the table with the other two, and plopped down into the caned seat. "Yum, baloney. Can I take the lettuce off?"

"Yes, honey, as long as you still eat it."

She joined us and poured lemonade into our glasses.

I sat and stared at Annie Maude, even as I ate my sandwich. Finally, she noticed and winked at me.

With that, I knew any questions about the chair wouldn't be welcomed.

"Are you excited to have a new baby brother or sister on the way?" she asked.

Jimmy stayed that weekend at Annie Maude's while his mother gave birth to his sister, Alice, at the hospital.

"Yeah, I *guess*," he said around a mouthful of sandwich. He wiggled in his seat like he couldn't get comfortable, and shrugged. "I'm just glad I don't have to wait at the hospital with Daddy."

I knew Annie Maude would say something about him talking with his mouth full.

But then…she didn't.

And what about the other rules? The chair! And, well…he had his elbows on the table—something she never allowed. She didn't even know about the window yet. I probably should have told her.

Well, if *he* could do it…. Taking another bite of my sandwich, I eased my elbows forward toward the tabletop. Grandma caught my eye and raised one eyebrow. That's all it took for me to sit up straight and focus on my lunch. Even so, my mind busied itself trying to understand how it was fair that I had to follow rules when my cousin didn't.

He squirmed in his seat, pushed it back some and sat on its edge.

"Jimmy, are you interested in stuff from the first world war?" Annie Maude asked.

"Who isn't?" he said, looking to me with a big goofy smile. "The fighting in the trenches was…."

His voice trailed off as I shrugged and turned up my nose.

Jimmy pushed his seat back further and stood while he finished his sandwich and downed his lemonade. Seemed maybe no one had ever sat in that chair for good reason. But who would know, just to look at it?

"Mr. McCary, next door, fought in World War One," Grandma said. "He has a great collection of trophies, things taken from the enemy. He's moving to an old soldiers' home and wants help cleaning out his attic. I told him you'd be here and might like to help. He said you could have whatever you found that you'd want, so long as it isn't dangerous."

"Yes, *Ma'am,*" Jimmy said eagerly, "*I'll* help him." His back went stiff and he saluted Annie Maude.

"I guess I'll help too." I droned the words to show a lack of interest.

"No, honey, we have our nap," Annie Maude said.

"Couldn't we skip it, just this once?"

"No, sweetheart, it's hot out and sweltering in that attic. That'll do you no good. Besides, you haven't been sleeping well. You need your rest."

How did she know? Silly question when she'd always known things about me I hadn't told her, most of them too small for my parents to bother mentioning to her either.

"Now that you've finished eating, you're already sleepy."

She was right. My head lolled forward a bit. I settled into myself with a heavy, lifeless feeling. I covered a yawn. Hauling dusty crap out of the old man's attic suddenly seemed the most unpleasant chore imaginable.

"Mr. McCary's house is the first on the left if you go out through the back porch," Annie Maude told Jimmy.

~ ~ ~

Soon as Jimmy headed out the door, my sleepiness lifted. Even though I'd just been thinking about how unpleasant the job would be, I became so miffed at having to take the nap, I could think of nothing but my cousin out having fun, exploring old man McCary's attic, probably finding better junk than Chet and me dug up from the riverbank. The best thing I ever found there was some old, stained dentures.

While I normally didn't get too upset about the naps, on that day they were stupid. Wanting to get it over with, I slid under Grandma's massive old bed a little too fast. My arm squeaked against the polished wood floor, and that burned—an injury to the insult.

Why did the underside of the bed have to be so clean? I'd never seen her clean there, and supposed that she must have done it on the weekdays, when

I wasn't around. Did she do that for me or for herself—who cared? I wouldn't have felt worse about it if the bed springs had been choked with cobwebs.

Grandma made her way in more slowly, with stiff movements. I'd been taking this mid-day, under-the-bed nap with her most weekends since first grade. I suppose I'd thought everyone took naps like that—that is until the day I'd said something about it to Chet.

We'd sat cross-legged on the braided rug in his room, trying to build a castle from toy logs. An ugly, brown castle for sure, but one that would still be fun to wreck with dinosaurs and slingshots.

"Hey, I got the new Mad magazine," Chet said, stretching to get the comic from the window seat.

Rain drummed against the roof.

"Yeah, I stole my brother's copy and hid it at Grandma's house." I took the comic from him eagerly and opened it. "I don't dare have it at home. If Mama saw….. Anyway, I didn't have a chance to get a look because Annie Maude and me stayed under the bed so long."

"Under the bed?" he asked, looking up from our castle.

"You know, a *safe nap*."

"Why under the bed?" Chet asked.

"Maybe in case there's a thunderstorm or a tornado," I said weakly, since I didn't really know.

"What are you talking about?"

I explained how Mama made us get under the bed in bad weather, and how I'd come to assume maybe Grandma had us napping there for a similar reason. The more I said about it, the more Chet frowned.

"What does that have to do with naps at your grandmother's house?"

"I don't know. Maybe Mama got the idea from her."

"That grandma of yours is something," he said, one finger circling his ear. "I don't want to say looney, but that's what I hear. They say that sort of thing runs in your family."

Of course, he referred to Mama.

He knew moms were off-limit, and he was supposed to be my friend! His goofy smile didn't let him off the hook for that.

I got in a huff and started to tear up. Ashamed to let him see me cry, I bashed the Lincoln-log castle, stomped out, and went home. I didn't speak to him again for a whole day.

That had been almost a year earlier.

I turned to look at my silent grandmother, wishing I could ask her questions about Jimmy, and fairness, and more questions about the queer nature of her rules. Looked like she'd fallen asleep. I had no way of knowing if Annie

Maude truly slept, yet I knew that if I made any move to get out from under the bed, her eyes would pop open, and fix sharply on my own.

And because I knew she wanted me to sleep, I resisted that very thing. My eyes tracing the patterns of the familiar steel coils above me, I pretended that busy little creatures lived there and went about their little ways, round and round. Occasionally, they'd look down at me and wave. Wanting to keep silent and still, I'd simply smiled back at them.

Maybe Jimmy would have stories to tell when he returned. Though not so fun as Chet, I liked having his company at our Grandmother's house.

Maybe Jimmy didn't have to follow the rules because he was a guest.

I'm *not a guest.* I *have my very own room here.*

I grew sleepy, even with a head full of questions.

~ ~ ~

"Lookit," Jimmy said, cornering me on the back porch. Carrying a ratty pillowcase the old man must've given him to carry his junk, Jimmy had returned from cleaning out Mr. McCary's attic. He held out a pale blue scrap of paper that bore a delicate green and pink flower pattern. "That's a piece of wallpaper from a World War One German dugout. They tried to make the dugouts homey, even though they were just part of the nasty, rat-infested trench system."

I knew little about World War One, but pretended interest, matching his wide-eyed look as he showed me his treasures.

Next out of the pillowcase came a small, stained flag, a scary eagle printed on both sides. "That's a lance pennant," Jimmy said. "Although they didn't wear armor, the Germans were still going into battle like knights on horseback with lances to stab the enemy with, our guys and the allies. The pennant would hang just behind the spear point. That brown stain is probably blood."

I frowned, thinking of all the horses that must have been harmed in the big shooting battles. They had no way to defend themselves.

He brought out a set of drumsticks, a moth-eaten military cap, and a gas mask in its canvas sack. He paused before showing his last treasure. "Mr. McCary said this one was a special gift for a young man." Jimmy made an exaggerated prideful face that looked goofy with his shit-eating grin.

I laughed so hard, I choked, and he thumped me on the back a couple times.

"He meant *me,* of course." Jimmy could hardly get the words out around his own laughter. He struggled to get serious. "Now listen, Mr. McCary said I shouldn't show anyone, but I'll let you see if you promise not to tell." His grin returned.

How could I say no? I imagined he'd show me something gross, like maybe a severed finger. Even so, I nodded.

Jimmy pulled out a small metal box, maybe two inches to a side, with a glass lens at one end, a frosted piece of glass at the other. "Hold the lens to your eye, and look toward the light."

The light coming through the box revealed a black and white image of a woman standing naked on some set meant to look Arabian maybe. She had on a feathered cape she held out to form wings, and a bunch of the same sorts of plumes stuck out from her butt crack. She had a big, naked bosom and a fat butt.

I laughed again, covered my mouth, and shoved the box back at Jimmy.

"You'd like it more if you were a boy," he said, taking the little box. "You'll keep it a secret, right?"

I nodded, still giggling. My face felt hot as I wondered if Jimmy wanted to look at *me* naked.

Annie Maude appeared in the doorway, and I saw Jimmy blush, deep red, all the way to his ears. He pocketed the small box right quick, and gave me a sheepish look.

Were my ears that red? I felt hot all over. Would Annie Maude notice?

She glanced at Jimmy, then at me, but said nothing.

Jimmy looked like he had to do something or burst. Finally, he said, "Oh," and reached for something in his back pocket. "I found something for you, too." He opened a thin leather wallet and handed it to me. Mounted in a paper frame inside, I saw a hand-colored photo of a little girl holding a rabbit. She looked a lot like Penny. Even her dress was pink. Though drawn to the ghost, I couldn't help being afraid of her. Now, it would be like I had an image of her that wouldn't be frightening.

"She looks just like you," Jimmy said. "And look, that could be your bunny." He pointed to the rabbit in the photo. "That's why I picked it."

I look like Penny? I got a better view of the face. *Maybe a* little.

I smiled and lifted the picture up so Annie Maude could see. She took the wallet and held it close.

"Mr. McCary said he took that off a dead German," Jimmy said. "It's probably the dead man's daughter, or something."

"Take all your stuff upstairs," Grandma said stiffly, "and wash up for dinner."

Jimmy clomped happily up the stairs.

I reached to take the wallet back. Annie Maude quickly put it in her pocket, and bent down to look me in the eye. "That's some dead man's sweet child."

"It's mine." I said.

She shook her head slowly.

I stomped the floor, suddenly angry with her for the first time ever. "Why can't I have it? It's not fair! You let Jimmy keep all that other stuff…" And then my words fell apart because what I wanted to say would have been unforgivable.

Even so, I bowed my head to see the stern look on Annie Maude's face. She cradled my chin in her hand, and got even closer. "The dead cling tightly to what they find precious. Mr. McCary is lucky if he never had a visit from that soldier."

Later, I would wonder what precious thing I had that belonged to Penny. Bunny? The chair beside the grandfather clock at home? Something more precious?

In that moment, though, I felt mistreated.

"Go wash up," she said. "Dinner is almost ready."

As I walked upstairs, I imagined the dead German soldier checking his pockets, looking everywhere for the photo. That made me uneasy. I defiantly stomped the rest of the way up the stairs, calling out to Jimmy, "Hey, dinner's ready, stupid!"

I stayed in the bathroom with the water running until the red had gone from my eyes, then went to join them.

~ ~ ~

"I have another secret," Jimmy whispered with toothpaste foam around his mouth, "one I have to tell you about."

We'd been told to get ready for bed, and stood in the bathroom brushing our teeth.

"Does it also have a big butt?" I giggled and toothpaste drooled out of my mouth onto my pajama shirt.

Jimmy spat in the sink, rinsed his mouth, and wiped his face with his pajama sleeve. "I saw Annie Maude bury something in a jar in her flower bed. The one between the persimmon tree and the shed."

That's where I'd been forbidden to dig. Annie Maude planted her shade-loving plants there, like bleeding hearts.

Jimmy tapped the Timex on his wrist. "About one o'clock this afternoon, I looked out the old man's attic window and saw her. She'd dug the hole, but before putting the jar in, she looked around all sneaky-like."

She had done that during our nap and I hadn't noticed. I ached to know what she'd put in that jar.

"That's weird," he said, "isn't it?"

"Maybe not for Grandma."

"Lights out," Annie Maude called out from her bedroom down the hall.

I rinsed my mouth and looked in the mirror at Jimmy. He had his finger on the light switch, waiting for me. I hesitated, wanting to say more.

"Goodnight," I said finally.

He flicked the light off and we headed to bed.

An hour later, in my socked feet and carrying my shoes, I found myself in Jimmy's room. Moonlight, slicing in through the single window, made a stripe across the floor that almost reached the bed. Setting my shoes on the floor, I knelt beside him.

I saw an opportunity. Though I wasn't there for Scare-a-boo, at that moment I knew I had him right where I wanted him. I took a few moments to savor my coming victory, and to think it through. If I startled him awake, he'd likely yelp, and awaken Annie Maude. I'd have to silence him somehow.

A giggle from the darkness on the other side of the bed. I clamped my mouth shut to keep from crying out.

How long had Penny been there? I'd never thought of her coming to Annie Maude's. Had she followed me?

As the moments passed, she made no move to show herself. Maybe she wanted to watch from the shadows.

Okay, then… Ready with my hand hovering over Jimmy's lips, I said, "Boo," into his ear and clapped the hand down over his mouth.

Jimmy made *mumphing* sounds so loud I thought surely Annie Maude would hear him. His hands went to his face. With my other hand, I struggled to stop him from freeing his mouth. Leaning over, my chest on his, I whispered, "Scare-a-boo, *got* you. Now, be quiet so Grandma doesn't hear."

He grew calm. I listened for any sounds coming from Annie Maude's bedroom. I glanced into the darkness where I thought Penny might be, unnerved to think Jimmy might find out about her. Not sure why. After a long, still moment, I removed my hand from Jimmy's mouth.

He wasn't smiling. "Yeah, you *got* me," he said, shoving me off him too hard. "You'd do *anything* to win *wouldn't* you?"

That hurt, and I thought maybe I'd gone too far.

Knowing he hated spiders, I said, "I wouldn't put a spider in your bed."

"I wouldn't put it *past* you."

I stood and folded my arms "Ok, what wouldn't *you* do?"

Jimmy thought for a moment, and smiled. "I wouldn't set your hair on fire." Lightning fast, he reached to tug on one of my pigtails and chuckled.

Another giggle from the darkness beyond his bed. Jimmy's head whipped around to face the voice. "Did you hear that?"

"What?" I pretended.

Jimmy looked at me, then frowned into the darkness. A moment later, he shook his head, as if denying what he'd heard.

Looking at the glowing green face of his watch, he said, "Not even eleven yet. Are you looney?"

I resisted the urge to punch him. He didn't know he shouldn't say that to *me*, of all people, considering Mama's troubles.

"Yeah, well, I'm not really here for Scare-a-boo," I said, bending to pick up my shoes. "You're gonna get up and help me find that jar you saw Annie Maude bury today."

"No I'm *not*! She'd kill us or put a curse on us. You know how she is."

"Yes, you *are*. Put your shoes on and come with me."

He sat up, folded his arms, and gave me a cold stare.

I almost laughed. "You afraid, Captain Scare-a-boo? After tonight, I don't think you can even compete in the same league as me"

"Oh, we've got Scare-a-boo leagues now, huh?"

"Well, just between you and me. Anyway, you're a pussy if you don't come help me."

His mouth became a hard line and he shut his eyes.

"Like I thought," I said, "you're just a *sweet*."

Jimmy opened one eye to squint at me. He grinned. "I suppose you're the one has to follow all her rules. I always get away with stuff."

I didn't know he'd noticed. Knowing that he had, I resented having to follow her rules even more. Well, I'd decided to break a big one, her first rule. Sounded like Jimmy had given in. He could think what he wanted. If we got caught, maybe I'd tell her that breaking the rules had been his idea.

"Let's go find out what's in that jar," I said. "Carry your shoes until we get to the back porch."

Jimmy swung his legs to the floor and bent to put on his socks. I looked again into the darkness for Penny. Nothing. I wanted to tell myself I'd imagined her.

The warmth of the late spring night allowed us to go out in our pajamas, mine with images of cowgirls on bucking broncos, his with finned rockets streaking between the stars.

I knew where the floorboards squeaked, the treads of the stairs being the worst, and we mostly avoided those spots, sometimes having to hop from one place to the next. The back porch door stuck a bit, but I got it opened with little rattling noise. We put on our shoes. I grabbed a couple of trowels from the bench outside, gave one to Jimmy.

We were in luck—the black shadow of the shed spread over the lawn, past the persimmon tree, almost to the house.

"This is nuts," he said.

"Yeah, it is."

"I can't even see."

Since I was such a night owl, I could see fairly well in darkness, so I led the way, dragging Jimmy by the hand. The top of the persimmon tree and the edge of the shed's roof in moonlight told me where to go. Getting close to the flower bed, I said, "Careful, there are rocks at the edge of the garden.

"I can see better now," he said, and shook his hand loose. "Look for the bare spot."

"Here," I said, and crouched down next to the recently disturbed soil.

"Yeah, that's it." He dropped down beside me.

I hesitated, wondering if I wanted to know the truth. Did Annie Maude get up to evil mischief, crimes even? Or was she simply crazy? Would I find some terrible secret just under the dirt?

Jimmy dug into the soil eagerly. He'd forgotten to be afraid. Almost immediately he hit the metal lid of a jar. He wrestled the glass vessel free and brushed off the loose soil. A white jar, like the ones in that awful cabinet in the cellar. I could barely see through the milky glass to the inside. In the dimness, I couldn't tell if it held anything. Jimmy unscrewed the lid, peered inside, then gave me a puzzled look.

"What?" I asked, and he handed me the jar.

"A toothpick," he said, sounding disappointed.

I reached inside, and pulled the slender piece of wood out. Yes, a toothpick. One end had been chewed, and it had the faint odor of cinnamon. I thought of the ones, soaked in cinnamon oil, that some kids at school sold.

My turn to be disappointed. My heart sank, thinking I'd just learned that all Annie Maude's rules and mysterious ways *were* lunacy, as Chet had suggested. Turning away from the idea, I began to dig.

"What are you doing?' Jimmy asked.

"There will be more."

With my bare hands, I dug and quickly found another jar. I had to tug the glass vessel loose from the soil. "The top's on too tight," I said, struggling. "Maybe it's been in the ground longer."

Jimmy took the jar from me and got it opened.

Looking inside, he said, "Some *treasure*."

"What?"

"A stupid spoon." he said, pulling the utensil out.

I recognized it as one of Annie Maude's fancy, silver jelly spoons.

What Chet had told me folks said about us was the truth, then—crazy ran in my family. That meant I might be crazy too.

My shoulders sagged, and I felt like I was sinking into the dirt. I didn't like what I'd discovered. We could rebury the jars, but I couldn't forget what they'd shown me.

Jimmy lifted another jar from the soil.

Though I told myself I didn't want to see any more, as he twisted the lid open, my curiosity got the better of me.

He reached in and pulled out a shiny amber jewel. Even in the gloom, I could see the scant light passing through its translucent yellow center. A piece of glass? Dirt from Jimmy's fingers stuck to it. He lifted the amber jewel to his nose, sniffed, and stuck out his tongue to get a taste.

"Eeewww," I said.

He looked at me. "Butterscotch. Looks like it's been sucked on."

Memory came with the sensation of choking. I coughed and gasped. "No!" I whispered. "It can't...."

I could see the confusion in Jimmy's eyes. How could I explain?

A long shadow appeared on the moonlit part of the lawn, stretching toward us—a man wearing a hat, moving through the alley behind the house.

"Quick," Jimmy said. He returned the candy to the jar. I heard it plinking around in there as he placed the container in the dirt next to the other two. We shoved the loose soil over all three jars and took off for the house.

Looking back, I saw the shadow retreating back the way it had come.

Determined to think no longer about what we'd found, I tried to keep my thoughts a jumble as we snuck back into the house.

I got in bed with unwanted thoughts of butterscotch: The taste, the smell, the experience of the hard sweetness slowly dissolving in my mouth.

And then the shadow of a man wearing a hat—why did it have to be more than that?

Trying to quiet my fears, I remembered Daddy's words as he and Mama spoke about the man who helped us the day I choked on the butterscotch. He'd asked Mama if she remembered a guy who showed up at the mill trying to sell his car. "The deal he offered was too good to be true," Daddy had said. "Something about him—I just knew he was a swindler."

He'd nodded when Mama asked, "You think the guy that helped us was a criminal of some sort?"

So maybe the man in the black fedora was a criminal and I'd sensed that somehow, like Daddy had with the car salesman. What were the chances that the man who helped me would be walking through the alley behind Annie Maude's house? Even if the same man, what were the chances he'd help me one time, but come back to harm me the next? Nope, had to have been someone out for a late-night stroll.

Before I knew it, sleep found me.

~ ~ ~

Annie Maude and I said our goodbyes to Jimmy mid-morning, Sunday. Before turning away to go to his father's car out front, he winked at me, as if to say, "we got away with it."

I wasn't so sure. Of course, Annie Maude had had plenty of time to deal with us both if she'd even suspected what we'd got up to in the night. She might not want to punish Jimmy. Me, on the other hand…I had to wonder if I should indeed be afraid of her.

I couldn't help thinking about the butterscotch candy we'd discovered. I still refused to do much more than remember seeing it in Jimmy's hand. I did not want to consider what it being in that jar meant.

Annie Maude closed the door and went back into the kitchen. I thought she'd start cleaning up after our late breakfast. Instead, she sat, said, "Sit with me."

Seeing what was coming, I tried and failed to think of excuses. She took my hand and gently guided me into the seat next to her. Nope, I hadn't gotten away with anything.

"I awoke to a terrible pain last night," Annie Maude said. She brushed crumbs from the table into her hand and dropped them onto her plate. "I put that toothpick in the ground for a reason."

She knew everything, down to the smallest detail. I cringed, thinking I was done for. Though cringing only inside, I knew I must look awful guilty on the outside.

She left a considerable silence between us, yet didn't seem to spend that time turning angry. Of course, Annie Maude didn't always wear her feelings on her face.

"A piece of that toothpick broke off in my gum last month, caused an abscess that took a couple of my teeth. Worst pain I ever had, except for giving birth to your mother."

The look on her face told me how angry she'd been to lose those teeth. She'd suffered all that without me knowing.

Grownups!

Then the strangest thing: she laughed, and pulled the corner of her mouth to one side so I could see the empty gums. She turned it into a goofy face.

Still uneasy, I didn't want to laugh. Even so, a chuckle escaped me.

She gave me her most pleasant smile. "I use the jars, like the ones you found in the garden, to help me live with memories that are difficult. The things held in the jars represent in some way those memories."

I must have been frowning in confusion. Annie Maude took my hands and squeezed them gently. "First, I bury the objects in the ground for a certain length of time. Some I leave buried for a *long* time. Once they're *done*, I dig them up and store the jars in the large cabinet in the cellar. This practice allows me to set aside painful events in my life so that I don't carry those burdens every day."

I had so many questions, but couldn't decide which ones to ask. I chose a simple one, not thinking the answer would be so important. "Why are the jars milky-white? You can barely see what's inside."

"They're white so I can't clearly see what's inside until I mean to. That way, the recollections remain distant until I choose to open them and face them in full light."

Whether I believed her or not, I could follow her meaning, much like I accepted the magic in a fairy tale.

She placed a knobby hand on one of mine, said, "You'll see for yourself soon enough. The little red cabinet in the cellar that tempts you so—that's your cabinet, a gift from me. It's filled with the same sort of jars. You will largely forget what you put in those jars, but you mustn't abandon the recollections entirely. You must look in the cabinet at least once a year and revisit all of them. That will help lessen the power they have over you, and give you a chance to decide which of them you are willing to accept and live with. Once you've visited the memories, they will persist for about a week before fading again."

I tried a skeptical look, thinking she might give me a knowing grin, and then I'd know she'd been kidding me about all the weird cabinet business.

Instead, she raised her brows in a sober expression, looked me squarely in the eyes, and nodded slowly.

I nodded to show I understood.

"The cabinet and jars have other powers too," she said. "I use some of mine to germinate hope and to help me learn from regret. Some hold agreements, contracts of sorts; those I have with myself, and ones I've made with other spirits."

I kept quiet for a long time, trying to hold what she'd told me loosely in my head. We sat silently, yet comfortably together.

"That's all you need for now," Annie Maude said. "We'll get to the rest later."

Giving her the benefit of the doubt, I'd decided that Annie Maude wasn't a lunatic. She did indeed bring some small, quiet magic into the world, and I would happily learn to do the same.

"So," I said finally, trying not to smile, "you're not angry with me for digging in your garden?"

"No. I knew you'd break the rules in a big way one day. The consequences are what you learned from what you found. That's no small thing for a child of your age."

The Butterscotch.

"That fellow in the black hat that scares you, he's the one that startled you two last night. He came because you unearthed that piece of candy. You'll want to be careful whenever he shows up."

Needing that man to remain some low-life who just gave me the creeps, I didn't ask how she knew of him, nor how she'd gotten the piece of butterscotch and why she'd put it in that jar.

Grandma seemed to see I wasn't up to talking about that. "I know, honey, I know. It's too much," she said, gripping my shoulder lightly. "All I'll say is that it's a good thing you sealed those jars back up and buried them right quick, especially that last one."

I shriveled up a bit in my seat as she spoke those words. Unfortunately, because I didn't ask my questions, my imagination had free rein. That wasn't much better.

Annie Maude gave me a warm hug, and sat back.

She caressed her cheek. "I'll have to go throw some more soil on those jars this afternoon. My jaw still hurts a bit."

"I'm sorry, Grandma." I bowed my head, upset to think I'd caused her pain.

She placed her hand under my chin and tilted my head up so I looked her in the eyes.

"One last thing," she said. "All the rules about the house are lifted. It's time you made rules for yourself. How you may do that at home will be between you and your parents, but here, I'll expect you to stand by what you say and do. All that said, I'd prefer you to not dig in my garden."

She had put me at ease and given me something to look forward to.

Haint Blue and Ruth of Boogerboo
1967

On just another summer day, Chet and I crouched low on the ground like cats, peering through a basement window between its heavy iron bars. Singing had drawn us. We'd been out in the field behind the old bakery gathering *rocket weeds*. They were wildflowers that, having gone to seed, had long, cigar-shaped pods. If you looped the stem around the base of the pod, and pulled quick, the pod would pop off and shoot up like a rocket. We'd dropped our bouquets of brown pods as fascination with the singers in the basement took hold.

We saw two men of similar stature; big and muscled. Scars formed complicated patterns across the black man's chest. The other one, pale as moonlight, had faded tattoos of sexy women on his thick forearms and shoulders. Both had clean shaven heads.

The bakery hired prisoners, and because of that, we'd been told not to go near the place.

"Jail birds, singing, huh?" Chet said with a chuckle.

The men sang lustily:

> "When downside is upside
> > a glance at the debil,
> turns outside to inside,
> > I got myself trouble.

Rhythmic, like a sea shanty, yet somber, the song reminded me of the ones Ruth sang while doing her most monotonous chores for Mama.

> "The deep-dark river it flows like time,
> > gotta get in 'fore it leaves me behind,
> but in that dark river, flowing like time,

I'll sink to the bottom, burdened with crime.

They tossed a huge, shiny ball of bread dough back and forth to the rhythm of their song.

"There's no time like the present,
        absent the fall
and no time like the present,
        no time at all."

Their muscles strained under the weight of the dough ball, which smacked against their bare chests, slick with sweat.

"Gross," we said in unison.

"Sweet bread?" Chet said. "More like *sweat* bread!"

"Yuck, and the hair!"

"Yeah, eat *that* bread, and you'll be pulling fur from between those horse teeth of yours."

I punched him. "At least I'm not *pigeon-toed*."

He ignored me. "And what's with those witchy words?"

"Maybe Ruth would know."

A third man, tall, thin, and barefoot, came into view. The other two stopped tossing and set the great dough ball on a heavily floured table. The new fellow had an elaborate "7" tattooed on his long neck and wore a green apron dusted with flour. He reached for something on a shelf any ordinary man would need a step stool to reach.

The white fellow with the girlie tattoos punched the dough ball. "Almost ready for you."

"Hey, Pretzel," The black man said over his shoulder, "get the loaf pans out."

The new fellow, Pretzel I presumed, flipped open a cabinet below the counter to his right. Then his leg reached inside.

Chet and I looked at each other, as if to say, "Can you believe this?"

Out came a stack of bread pans, all held in the toes of Pretzel's right foot.

"No," I said, "I can't believe it."

"You have to, 'cause I see it too."

"That never gets old," girlie tattoos said. He picked up the dough ball and chucked it to the black fellow, and the song began again.

Pretzel turned away to work on the bread pans.

"See those scars on the black man?" Chet asked.

I squinted through the sooty window. Between tosses, I caught glimpses.

The scars looked like those I'd seen in Will's book of African tribesmen, a favorite of his because it had pictures of naked people.

"Those are vevè," Chet said.

"What's that?"

"They're voodoo symbols, used to draw spirits to you or send them away. I saw pictures in our encyclopedia. If Ma knew they were in there, she'd toss out the whole set. Then I'd be in *voodoo do-do* the next time I had to look something up."

I covered my mouth to stifle my giggles. Chet elbowed me in the side and gave me a big grin.

"Doesn't she know there's good magic too? There's voodoo, and then there's hoodoo. My grandma helps people with her magic. Ruth does too."

"Well, don't let Ma hear about it."

"That song might be some magical chant," I said. "If I sing it to Ruth, maybe she'll tell me what it means."

"If we sing along, it'll stick with us."

We began to sing. The words and rhythm contagious, we got caught up in it, raising our voices, swaying and nodding to each other. Chet picked up some sticks and beat the rhythm on the window bars.

"Hey you!" came a voice from inside. The singing stopped. Pretzel's face, grinning a mouth full of gold teeth, looked out at us. "You little shits, you wanna sing too? Come on in!" He pressed his lips to the dirty glass with a big sloppy kiss.

I shrieked, and grabbed Chet. He fell back. We scrambled to our feet. I grabbed up our rocket weeds and followed Chet, running toward the street. The convicts' laughter followed us longer than I thought it should. By the time we reached the road, we were laughing too.

As we headed for home along the gravel edge, Daddy's Nova cruised toward us. He stopped the car, reached over to roll down the window on the passenger side. "I thought you wanted to go to Ruth's with me."

Chet and I leaned into the window.

"I forgot!" I said. "Can Chet come?"

"If he'd like to. What do you say, Chet?"

"No way. Ma would skin me alive if I went to BoogerBoo."

Daddy took a second look at Chet. "You okay son? You look a little green around the gills."

I stepped back to see what he meant. Chet did look pale and sweaty.

"Just hot from running, is all."

He appeared uneasy, and I chalked that up to him not wanting Daddy to know we'd been watching the convicts.

I gave the rocket weeds to Chet, said my goodbyes, and got in the car. We drove slowly to the black part of town, *Boogerboo,* as the place was crudely called. At Ruth's house, I helped Daddy unload the paint and the step ladder.

"Lord, there you both be," Ruth said, coming out to greet us. "How're you doing on this fine Saturday?"

"Fair to middlin', thanks." Daddy pried the top off the paint can with his pocketknife. "What do you say, Rooster?"

"I want to see the chickens. Can I feed them, Ruth?"

"No, done fed them, but we can walk in the back garden to visit."

Stirring the paint, Daddy said, "That *is* a pretty blue you picked, Ruth."

"Haint blue," she said, her eyes twinkling.

"Looks blue to me." He gave an exaggerated wink.

Ruth burst out with a hearty laugh. "Halloween could come ever day once you put that up."

"We just doing the ceiling?"

"That's all it takes."

Daddy unfolded the ladder, and took a measuring look up under the porch roof. "That ceiling's awful high," he said, rubbing his stubbly chin and turning to Ruth. "How 'bout *I* paint it. I don't relish the idea of you on that ladder."

Ruth smiled like she knew he'd say that, said, "I'll take all the help I can get."

Daddy pulled a pack of cigarettes from his pocket and tapped one out. He winked at me, and lit his cigarette. His movements, graceful and efficient, always drew my attention. Until then, I hadn't noticed he already wore his painting pants.

Ruth took up a basket. "Come on, girl, let's go see what that old Foghorn's up to."

We turned the corner around the south side of her house. The sunlight, coming through the trees like magic, lit up the colors of her garden: the flowers, the dancing butterflies, and faeries of drifting cottonwood fluff.

"Blessed be this glorious morning, child," Ruth said, raising her arms like she accepted the beauty as a gift from heaven.

Even so, I knew the garden's enchantment came from Ruth—her joy at the world around her. She loved life and life gave that right back to her. Or had she cast a spell on me?

"Your garden's magic is *sure* different from Grandma's," I said.

Annie Maude's garden had its own beauty and a more tamed appearance—lots of rectangles—and had magic hidden beneath the surface. Ruth's garden, a much wilder growth, wore its charms on the outside. I did wonder if hers, too, had things hidden under the ground.

Ruth looked troubled that I'd brought up Annie Maude. Whenever they met, she and Grandma always spoke carefully to one another, handling their words like broken glass. Not because of dislike. No, they repulsed each other the way magnets did if turned a certain way; not by choice, but by some law of nature that demanded obedience. I had a feeling that wasn't the way things had always been between them. They both had mysterious ways, and they loved us. I loved them both, yet no room felt quite right with both of them in it.

Ruth placed a hand on my shoulder. "Yes, it is different," she said after a time.

"How?" I asked.

Again, she looked uneasy. "Annie Maude's work has to do with our heads and hearts. I heal the rest of the body."

"*Is* it magic?"

"Some people think so."

"Is it bad?"

"Some people think so." Ruth frowned and her lips made a hard line. "We mean no harm, but sometimes mistakes are made. Your Annie Maude—" She shook her head, closed her eyes and put a hand to her forehead.

Somehow, I knew she'd been thinking about a mistake Annie Maude had made. I couldn't imagine Grandma making a mistake.

Finally, she looked at me with a smile.

"Is it Voodoo?" I asked.

"Why would you ask that?"

"I don't know, just wondering about magic. Me and Chet heard a song about a dark river. One of the fellows singing it had scars on his chest, like fancy symbols. Chet said they were veve' and the song might be voodoo."

Ruth placed a hand on her hip, cocked her head to one side and asked, "Where did that boy ever hear of such things?"

"The encyclopedia."

"Well now I've heard it all!" Ruth let go with a belly laugh, bending over and slapping her leg.

With her laughing at what I had to say, I decided not to recite the song for her. She hadn't answered my questions anyway, just stepped around them. Like most adults, Ruth did that when she thought I was too young to handle the honest truth. I didn't hold that against her.

She arched her back and stepped farther into her garden, then motioned for me to join her between rows of sunflowers. The tall stalks, with their scraggly leaves and giant yellow flowers, towered over us, reaching for the bright sky.

Ruth pointed to a plant growing all on its own not far away, one with cascades of large white bell-shaped flowers. "This beauty here is called angel's trumpet. Some folks say it be poison. Most medicine *is* poison, if you don't know how to give it and how to take it. Understand?"

I nodded. The flowers looked like ruffled ball gowns. I couldn't help wondering what might be buried beneath the plant to make its blossoms so white, and I thought of Annie Maude's milky white jars.

"I don't think you do," she said, lifting my chin with a finger. "Where's your mind today, girl?"

"Ruth, does your garden have jars underneath?"

"No. I don't bury anything but bulbs and seeds…*and children who don't listen.*"

My eyes cut to hers.

"Just making sure you heard me." she said. And though she laughed, there was an uncomfortable edge to it. "Your Grandma told you about her jars, did she?"

Her smile had faded, and her eyes became serious, as if a dark cloud passed behind them. She paused and I could tell she considered saying something, perhaps about that mistake Annie Maude had made, and I suspected she might tell me what had come between them. I could also see that Ruth decided against it and then said, "You been seeing a man dressed all in black?"

I didn't want to answer that, and had the weirdest thought: Did Ruth and Annie Maude know about him because Mama had something to do with the man, something Daddy didn't know about? My ears roared and my chest tingled like when I'd gotten too close to the edge at Flat Rock Falls.

No, I would not think about him. We were talking about Grandma and her jars. "*What* did my Grandma *do?*"

Ruth's eyes got bigger than I'd ever seen them. She tried to take my hands into her own. I gently pulled them away.

Turning her eyes to the ground at our feet, she said, "Let's just say that no good comes from bargaining with that fellow. Whatever you do, don't talk to him. You do and he'll never leave you be."

So there, she'd as much as said he was a terrible swindler.

"I don't want to talk about him," I whispered.

She hadn't answered my last question. Asking her again would only irritate her.

Ruth looked at me, took a long, shuddering breath, and forced a smile. "This garden here is different in moonlight than in sun. Some of the flowers open at night." She gestured toward lily beds, and jasmine growing up into a small dogwood. "The air fills up with the smells—like secrets. Most folks is asleep then. But them that don't sleep, they come. The night blooming flowers are for them. The blue paint keeps them haints out of my house."

I swallowed hard once, and then again. Without looking at her, I asked softly, "like...like Penny?"

"Oh, child," she said, covering her face with her hands. "You do test me."

I raised my voice a bit, "*Them* that don't sleep—is Penny one of *them*?"

Clearly rattled, Ruth let out a long sigh. "Enough, she said, a little too sharply. She placed her hands firmly on my shoulders. "I'll not have it, child. That's your grandmother's business. You need to ask her."

I couldn't see me asking Grandma about Penny.

Thinking Ruth had become angry, my eyes filled with tears.

I heard Daddy's whistling. Any moment, he'd be coming around the corner to paint the little square ceiling over the back porch. The familiar tune spoke of his contentment, miles away from the chasm Ruth and I had been peering into. Sure enough, he appeared, hunched over with the ladder perched on one shoulder, the paint and brush in his other hand.

As he set the ladder down, I wiped my eyes with my shirt just in time. He stood and greeted us with a broad smile.

Ruth placed her arm around me, bent, and kissed the top of my head. She wasn't angry with me, after all.

Daddy liked painting, even overhead. Looking from him to Ruth and back again, I got the idea that he'd done this many times before, that the joke about "haint" blue was nothing new, and that the petals and cottonwood fluff drifting in the wind were persistent as time. Like they'd always done, the chickens clucked and scratched at the ground, and the smell of disturbed soil found me along with the fragrance of the flowers.

Watching him put the last few strokes on, Ruth said, "Well, that'll keep 'em out til next time." She seemed to consider what remained of the paint and glanced at me. "Maybe you should use the rest at your house."

Daddy chuckled. "I don't think so. Already, the choir director at church calls us 'The Addams Family.' I may be hanging onto my deaconship by a thread. I'd better not push my luck."

"I might find something to paint with it," I said.

A wind came up, catching a few wiry tendrils of gray hair that had escaped Ruth's headscarf.

"I think we gonna have us some weather," she said. She shaded her eyes with one of her long hands and peered through the trees at dark clouds in the distance. Seeing the wrinkles on her pale palm, I realized for the first time that Ruth had grown old.

The air felt a little colder. The chickens, including Foghorn, had retreated into the roost and gone quiet.

"All right then," Daddy said, "get your paint can and let's go."

On the way home, the sky darkened. Daddy turned on the headlights.

"Can I paint my bed haint blue?" I asked. Daddy chuckled, flicked his cigarette out and rolled up the window. The first fat drops spattered the windshield.

"Your bed…you want a haint blue bed?"

"I sure do like that color, Daddy."

~ ~ ~

I caught up with Chet at his house the next day. He came out back with our rocket weeds, and we sat on the swings. I set mine to swinging, but he just sat there.

Both he and the weeds looked too limp to be any fun.

"You're still poorly, ain't you?"

"Yeah," he said. "Wrap my arm around my head, pull, and it'd pop right off, just like one of those weeds. Wouldn't fly very far, though."

"Probably go higher than those pods we got yesterday would. They're hopeless."

Chet looked at the limp weeds in his lap, tossed them in the dirt, and brushed his hands on his pants.

I stopped my swing, said, "Maybe you should go to the doctor."

"That's against our religion. I'd have to be on my last leg for Mama to take me to a doctor. She hates them, calls them all quacks. She's got me on prayers and orange baby aspirin. Makes me feel like a sissy."

"What do you mean? I *love* those. They're delicious. I sneak them sometimes or say I need them, even when I don't, so Mama will give me some."

"Well, you *are* a sissy."

"Chet," shouted Mrs. Boyd from the back door. "Come on in. You're too sick to be out there."

She disappeared inside and Chet made no move to get up.

He leaned toward me and said, "'Cause you always got those dark circles under your eyes, Mama thinks you're sickly."

"Am not!" He didn't know how little I slept.

"She says *you* gave me the crud."

I balled my fist to punch him, but he looked too pitiful for that.

His mother appeared in the doorway again, her arms crossed and looking none too pleased. "*Chester* Boyd!"

"I'd better go in. We'll get some more rocket weeds when I'm feeling better tomorrow."

I walked him to the door, his mother watching us.

"Lucy, Chet should spend the next couple of days in bed, so no visiting." She turned away.

Chet leaned toward me again. "See you tomorrow behind the bakery at 11:00."

~ ~ ~

I left home with enough time to get to the old bakery by at least eleven o'clock. With the memory of Pretzel's slobbering lips against the glass, I wanted to stay out of sight in the tall grasses behind the building. I picked a couple of the rocket weeds, yet my heart wasn't in it, so I sat on the prickly ground where I could see the path Chet would take. Still, I kept one eye on the bakery window. I held up my hand and framed the window between my thumb and forefinger: the rectangle appeared about an inch tall from where I sat, so I guessed I'd be about an inch tall to anyone looking out and I had all that tall grass to help hide me. I tried to sing the song and couldn't remember the tune, but the words would stick with me forever:

> When downside is upside
> > A glance at the debil
> Turns outside to inside
> > I got myself trouble.

I know this.

While the song was new to me, the feelings were familiar. I marveled at the thought, convinced that I knew in my bones what "downside is upside" felt like, and what it meant to draw just that sort of "trouble" down on myself. The window, though made small by distance, looked menacing. I couldn't stop glancing at the dark rectangle as I watched the road for the familiar figure of my friend. Clouds moved in from the East, darkening the edge of the field. A cooler wind stirred the weeds around me. I decided to head back toward home in hopes of meeting Chet on the way. He was never late and usually arrived before me.

The walk back seemed much longer, somber under the darkened sky. By the time I reached the house, thunder rumbled faintly in the distance.

Reaching the back door, I noticed the paint can on the porch where I'd left it. Daddy hadn't stowed it, and maybe that meant I'd get to have a haint blue bed. I'd ask him again when he got home from the mill. That lightened my mood a little. I told myself that Chet would be okay, that maybe he just couldn't sneak away.

The scent of laundry starch and faint sounds from our television met me as I opened the door. Ruth ironed in the living room. She seemed different in our house than she did standing in her garden, like she'd stepped out of herself somehow. All the same, her eyes turned warm when she saw me.

"Your Mama went with Aunt Jimmy to get her hair done. She waited awhile to see if you wanted to go with her, but had to go on to get to the appointment." She clipped one of Mama's skirts to a hanger, turned to the next piece of clothing.

A flash of light and a boom of thunder. We both jumped, then laughed.

"Oh Lordy," she said, "that one pro'bly ran my chickens in." She unplugged the iron, and stepped over to turn the television off.

I plopped down on the couch, and she took the chair across from me.

"Samiches for lunch," she said. "I don't trust that stove for nothin' in a thunderstorm."

"Ruth, why doesn't Grandma paint her porch ceilings blue?"

Thunder boomed again, and I got off the couch to sit by Ruth's feet. The rain started full and heavy.

"Use to, but not anymore."

I thought of Penny in the dark corner of Jimmy's room. I didn't like that.

"Is that why you and Grandma don't like each other?"

Ruth sat up straighter, leaned toward me. "Child. I love your Annie Maude, and I believe she loves me too. But we had us a falling out. She nor I can bring ourselves to talk about what come between us, so it just hangs there, heavy. Neither one of us wants to touch it for fear of the hard feelings crashing down on us all, your mama especially."

I thought she meant Mama was too fragile for that.

"Was it about…haints…Penny?"

Ruth winced. She glanced around the room, into shadows and doorways. "Let's don't talk about those things here," she whispered.

Loud and steady, the rain beat down outside. The air felt heavy and damp, just the sort of thing folks said made people sick, and just what Chet didn't need right then. My worries about him grew.

"Ruth, Chet's very sick and his mother won't take him to the doctor." I don't know why I whispered my words. "Do you think you could make him some medicine? I never saw him this sick before. He's got a fever and a terrible cough. He's all sweaty, and Daddy says his gills are green."

Ruth seemed to smile to herself.

"I know what that means," I said in a huff, even though I wasn't sure I did.

"Yes, child, I'll make him up something soon as I get home."

The thunder boomed again.

"Why don't you go fetch your brother from his secret lair. He might be doin' some Frankenstein stuff in there. Make him wash his hands." She made a yuck face. "Then you wash up too."

~ ~ ~

I tried to entertain myself after lunch, but with the rain keeping me indoors, I just stared out the window and worried about Chet. When I couldn't stand the waiting without knowing any longer, I tried calling his house.

"He's too ill to come to the phone," Mrs. Boyd said.

That seemed awful sick.

I tried cutting out paper dolls and scaring them with monsters from collector's cards Will had given me. All I could think of was how much more fun that would be with Chet.

I had to go check on him.

The rain had slackened to a drizzle. Through the kitchen window, I saw a strip of blue sky in the distance headed our way.

"I'm going to see about Chet," I called as I headed out.

"You put your raincoat on," she said, "and stay out of puddles."

On the back porch, I shook my raincoat so Ruth would hear and think I'd put it on. I left it on the hook and went out.

At Chet's, I stood in the back yard looking up at his bedroom window, wondering how to talk to him. The dark clouds had returned. I saw no light coming from his room. His mother's car sat in the driveway, and I knew she wouldn't let me in. I got closer to the house, directly under his window and gathered up pebbles from below the gutter downspout. Stepping back a ways and throwing them one at a time, I hit the glass twice.

A light came on. A surge of hope.

His mother's silhouette appeared. I dashed toward the house to keep her from seeing me. I had to get out of there before she came to look.

Cutting through the hedge into their neighbor's yard, I got to the alley and ran home, the rain chasing me. The storm caught up and I got drenched.

I dripped my way through the house, calling out for Ruth and getting no answer. The clock in the kitchen said 4:10.

I'd just lost track of time. Daddy must have come and gone with Ruth already.

Ruth had said she would prepare something for Chet soon as she got home, so that's where I had to go. If I asked Daddy to take me when he got back, he'd want to know why, and I didn't want to tell him I'd asked her for magic. Besides, he'd probably pick up Mama at her hair appointment before returning, and I couldn't wait. Getting to Ruth's house on foot, five miles away, would take some doing, yet I had to try. I changed into dry clothes. My tennis shoes were hopelessly soaked and muddy, and I didn't want to wear my good shoes inside my galoshes. I decided to put the galoshes on my socked feet. Donning my raincoat, I pulled the hood up, and headed out the back door.

Not wanting to run into Daddy along the roads, I took one of the trails that wandered along the river. The rain had stopped. My raincoat protected me from what dripped from the trees. I heard the swollen river, sometimes near, sometimes farther away. A feeling of confidence came over me with a sense that I pursued an important mission. I picked up my pace, running at times.

My galoshes began to rub a sore spot on the heel of my right foot, followed quickly by the same on my left foot. I had to slow down. Even then, I could feel both sores getting worse. Still, my determination didn't waver. I stopped to sit on a log and pull my socks up inside the galoshes. The wind blew my hood off and I pulled the strings to cinch it up tight around my face. I moved on, ignoring the pain in my feet.

The woods grew darker. I jumped at a blinding flash and the great peal of thunder that came with it sent me cowering down on the trail. Once up again, I ran in sheer fright. The pain in my heels slowed me before too long.

Then, all the rain came down at once, like a giant faucet had been turned on, right over me. I saw little but the flooded trail, and thought maybe the river had overflowed. My right foot sank into a puddle so deep the water overtopped my galosh. The flow inside cooled the growing blister on my heel. That felt so good, I wanted the same for my other foot. When I tried to lift my leg from the puddle, the mud held on and pulled the galosh off. I crouched to retrieve the rubber shoe. The thing let go suddenly, smacking me in the face hard and throwing mud in my eyes. Tilting my head back so the rain could wash the mud away, my hood fell back and cold water rushed down my shirt.

I sat to put my galosh back on. That felt like a cold bath.

What am I doing?

I imagined myself warm and dry, sitting in front of the heater at home. Mama and Daddy wouldn't have to know I'd turned it on.

No, I had to get help for my best friend.

I got up and trudged on.

~ ~ ~

I feared becoming lost in Boogerboo. The houses *did* look familiar—all had the same sharp-peaked roofs, skinny chimneys, and the weathered, broad clapboard of Ruth's house. But where was her garden and chicken coop? Having already mistaken two hen houses for hers and entered strangers' yards, I feared coming upon someone and startling them. Had I taken the wrong trail? I knew the way, yet in the dim light and rain, the area seemed unfamiliar.

Backtracking, I took a turn onto a trail that led away from the river, and seemed to get my bearings. I knew those cottonwoods along that curve of the trail. Ruth and I had picked blackberries there the summer before.

Seeing her chicken coop, with its tin roof rusted red, I began to run, calling Ruth's name.

I dashed through the split in the back hedge, then slipped and fell in the chicken yard. Pebbles, hard corn kernels, and dung stuck to me all over.

Ruth stepped from her back porch and hurried to help. "Lordy, child, What's happened? Are you hurt?"

She picked me up and hauled me in the house quick. I never felt more relieved.

Ruth set me on my feet on the linoleum floor of her kitchen, grabbed a towel, and began wiping at my face. A moment passed and she pulled back to get a better look at me. "Lord, child," she said, her voice shrill and broken, "someone after you? Who give you that black eye and bloody nose?"

I put my hand to my face and felt around my eye—a bit sore, yet the skin didn't feel black. My hand came away red. I looked at my feet, said quietly, "Did it to myself. No one else."

Clearly relieved, Ruth sagged a little. She shook her head and clucked, smiling. "That must have took *some* doing. Shoo-wee. Don't you be spreading that pea gravel and chicken scat all over my kitchen—stay put 'til I get a bath ready."

Ruth stepped into the bathroom. I heard the squeaky faucet and water running. "Your parents know where you are?"

"Of course they don't," we said at the same time.

"Jinx," I said.

She chuckled.

"What in the Sam Hill are you doin here, girl?"

"Did you make it yet?"

"Make what?"

"The medicine for Chet!" I said angrily. "You said you'd make it when you got home. That's why I come. He's too sick to wait." I wiped away tears before she saw them.

Ruth stepped out of the bathroom. "I hadn't got 'round to it, but if you'll go in and wash, I'll get my needs and work on it."

I did as she asked. Ruth came in after I'd undressed and gathered up my clothes and galoshes.

"I'll put these filthy things out to rinse in the rain."

The bath water had leaves and God-knows-what-else mixed in, like some giant cup of tea. I noticed insect wings—maybe wasp—several sets of them floating on top. "Oh well," I said aloud, and forced myself to get in, relax, and enjoy the warmth. I trusted Ruth to know what was good for me.

First, I washed my hair, then twisted it inside a thin towel that had blackbirds embroidered delicately at the hem.

I considered Ruth's bathtub the eighth wonder of the world. I'd meant to ask her about it before and always forgot. The thing was deeper than I'd imagined. I would worry about falling asleep in something that big. I tried to figure out how the tub came to be in that tiny bathroom—certainly it couldn't have passed through the narrow doorway. My fingers traced the tub's sculpted, enameled edge. I leaned out to get another look at the fancy bronzed legs that ended in claws.

Though she'd shut the bathroom door, I heard her bustling about in the kitchen.

The tub faced a small window set high in the wall. Glass bottles of various shapes and colors lined the sill. Even the weak light of the rainy day illuminated them, painting the walls in stained glass glory. In my birded turban, in the fancy, exotically scented tub, I felt a little princess-like.

Disgusted at the thought, I sat up straight, remembering why I'd come.

Ruth came in and handed me a cup. A curl of steam rose from the liquid within, and an earthy, aromatic smell. I opened my mouth to protest, but she gave me that look of hers, and I drank the thick, licorice-tasting liquid down. Not so bad, after all. Must have had a touch of honey. She sat on the edge of the tub and pulled what looked like a doll from her apron pocket, one fashioned from twigs, herbs, bones, and narrow strips of fabric. The thing smelled much like what I'd just swallowed, only worse.

"A wishbone?" I recognized the shape, having pulled many a wishbone with Will at the end of Sunday dinners. He always won.

I reached for the bone.

Ruth pulled the doll away. "Yes," she said. "You mustn't touch it. I can because I made it." She wrapped her creation in a square of cloth and placed that in a paper bag.

"You will take this little guy to your Chet. Do *not* open it. Do *not* play with it. You are to lay it under his bed, unfold the cloth, and leave it *undisturbed* until he's better. Do you understand my instructions?"

"Yes," I said, nodding uncertainly. She made the task sound as dangerous as the hauling of nitroglycerin in that western Will and I had watched on TV days earlier.

"*Do* you understand my instructions?"

"*Yes*," I said with more confidence.

Ruth put the wrapped-up doll back in her pocket and stood. She walked away and came back with folded clothes.

"These belonged to my boy. They'll have to do until we get you home. I don't know how you're gonna explain this to your Daddy. Gives me a headache just thinking about it."

The rain had slowed to a drizzle. The light through the window brightened.

"I'd better head back," I said. "But before I put those galoshes back on, I need bandaids for the blisters on my feet."

"Look at them now."

I pulled first my right, then my left foot up so I could see. To my astonishment, the blisters were gone. I looked my question at Ruth. She gave me a knowing smile, and shrugged.

"You ain't going back the same way you come." Ruth chuckled, and shook her head. "I called your house. Will says he don't know when your folks will be home. They went out to dinner, and a movie. He's cookin' for you both. You're to get home 'Forthwith.' Yeah, he did say it that way."

I rolled my eyes.

"I got some shopping to do," Ruth said. "I'm making a noodle salad for church tomorrow. My neighbor is taking me to the Red and White. We can take you home on the way."

"Ruth…" I'd planned to thank her, but "…your bathtub!" came out instead.

She chuckled again. "Ain't it something?" She ran her hands over its smooth enameled rim, like I had.

"It belongs in a castle," I said.

"The tub was a gift from that fellow we spoke about yesterday."

"You mean the one with the fedora?"

Ruth nodded. "It's too big, and too heavy—my son had to build up the floor under the house to hold it. I accepted the gift without thinking—a younger woman's foolishness—and many a time since, regretted it. It *is* a joy to soak my old bones in, for sure."

Her smile faded and she gave me a mock-stern look. "Now, get dry and dressed. Ain't got no shoes for you, but I'll dry your rubbers best I can." She stood to leave the room.

"Why do you regret it," I asked, "the tub?"

"Don't matter now." Ruth said through gritted teeth. She leaned forward to adjust my bird towel turban, looked me in the eye. "Every gift carries a debt. There're some beings you just don't want to be beholden to." She turned and left the bathroom, closing the door behind her.

He'd cheated her somehow, and I knew better than to ask her about it.

I felt a pressing urge to get out of that damned tub. I dried, dressed, and left that room not a moment too soon.

~ ~ ~

Mr. Johnson's truck rattled and put-put-putted, and his windshield wipers left arching smears across the glass, but the clunker got me home. I'd sat between them all the way, chewing my lip and worrying over being found out. I wore my raincoat and galoshes over the borrowed clothes. No socks this time, so my feet squelched in the boots. My heels didn't hurt anymore. Thankfully, no car sat in our driveway. Ruth got out of the truck. I thanked Mr. Johnson and hugged Ruth, carefully taking the magic doll in its paper bag.

"Remember what I told you," she said, then climbed back up onto the seat, and closed the door. They rattled off down the street. I heard Mr. Johnson's laugh, deep and rich, fading into the distance.

Soon as they were out of sight, I made a beeline to Chet's house—no time to lose.

Coming up the alley behind their house I hesitated at the hedges, long enough to get a nose full of the garbage can smell. I peered between wet leaves at the house. Because the storm clouds had passed on by and the sky had brightened, I couldn't see any lights on. No car in the drive. I went to the back door and knocked quietly. No answer.

The door swung open when I tried the knob.

"Hello?"

Again, no answer.

Upstairs, I found Chet lying on his side, his back to me, the covers pulled up around his shoulders. He shivered and his breath came a little raspy. I quietly knelt and pulled the cloth-wrapped doll from the bag, slid the whole thing under his bed, and carefully unfolded the cloth without touching the figure. The doll lay flat, staring upward, and I thought of grandma and me, lying under her bed.

I tiptoed down the stairs, let myself out and closed the door behind me.

"Every gift carries a debt," Ruth had told me. That came to mind as I thought about all I'd gotten away with that day through the gift of luck. I'd have to be extra good for a while, until I'd paid back what I owed to lucky chance. By the time my parents returned from all their errands, I was home, in my pajamas, on my bed, reading as though I'd been there for hours. I'd dried my raincoat and galoshes, and left them on the porch where they belonged.

~ ~ ~

The next morning, Sunday, I came downstairs and gobbled a bowl of cereal. I heard one of those badly-dubbed, Italian Hercules movies playing on the television in the living room, and knew Will must be up too.

Eager to see what the magic doll had done, I dressed and headed back to Chet's house. Like before, the car was gone.

This time, the doorknob didn't turn. Hesitating, yet still determined, I knocked gently.

The door opened and a cloud of that burnt-leaf smell wafted out. Chet's dad appeared, wreathed in smoke.

"Well now, speak of the devil," he said, a wide grin on his face. Then he bowed deeply and gestured, showman-like, for me to come in. His eyes were squinty and red, his long hair tousled. Like Will had said, a single strand of tiny beads hung around his neck.

"Go on up," he said, "but don't stay long. You'll need to skedaddle before the missus gets back. Or you and me both will have hell to pay. I don't know what you did *this* time, but that woman's got a *mad* on her, Miss Lucy."

Did she know I snuck in yesterday? Had I been caught? My cheeks grew hot at the thought and I dashed up the stairs to Chet's room.

"How'd you get in," he asked, "and what happened to your eye?"

"I fell," I lied, and shrugged. "Your dad let me in."

He struggled to sit up against the headboard. If anything, he looked worse than the day before. "He did?" Chet asked.

"Yeah."

"Huh…? Yesterday Ma found a Voodoo doll under my bed. Did you do that?" He smiled, asking, "Did you *voodoo* me?" Chet seemed impressed.

I bent and looked under the bed. "It's gone—did your ma—?"

"Yep, and boy-howdy did she ever stomp around and holler. She took it outside and threw it in the bin, yellin' all the way. Heard her slam the lid down. Probably they heard her all the way in Africa, where voodoo came from!" Chet doubled over in a coughing fit, snagged some tissue from a box on the bedstead and wiped his nose and eyes. "First thing this morning, she went out in a huff, saying she was off to talk to your Annie Maude. She pulled out so fast, gravel hit the house, and Dad yelled, 'Go ahead, just tear it all up,' though there was no way she heard."

I turned to go get the doll from the trash.

"Wait," he said, "listen to this. Ma's fingers were black from touching the thing. Wouldn't wash off for nothing."

I hope she didn't ruin it.

"Be right back," I said and headed downstairs. Outside, I ran to the alley, fearing the doll might be gone. Lifting the lid, I breathed a sigh of relief and immediately regretted it. Seemed like I could actually taste the garbage. Wadded in the cloth, the little guy lay atop the trash in sorry shape; one of the arms cracked and ready to fall off, the wishbone dislodged and dangling from the chest. I tugged the cloth up so I could grip the doll between the fabric, then blew coffee grounds off its head.

Returning with it to the house I saw Mr, Boyd, Chet's dad, standing in the doorway, shaking his head. "Oh no you don't, uh uh," he said. "Sorry, kid, no can do. You'd better put that right back where you found it. Go on home and stay away for a while, if you know what's good for you…and for me. You want us both to get scalped?"

Rock and roll music played somewhere in the house. Mr. Boyd never went to church.

He watched me. I turned, crossed the lawn to the alley, lifted the garbage can lid, and made a show of slamming it down. He seemed satisfied and went inside.

I ran home with the doll tucked in my pocket.

Now what? Church would start in less than an hour. I needed an idea and I needed one quick.

I couldn't go to Grandma—she would be getting an earful from Chet's mother. I pictured her yelling at Annie Maude from inside of one of her jars, as Grandma screwed the lid down tight. That might've made me laugh if I hadn't been so worried about Chet. He'd be calling this "some deep doo-doo."

I needed a strategy—this was war.

Jimmy! He'll help!

Hope lightened my heart and quickened my pace.

Since Mama could read me like an open book, I paused on the back porch, leaned over to put my hands on my knees, taking in deep breaths and trying to calm myself so her suspicions wouldn't be raised.

Inside, Mama stood before the hall mirror, putting on gloves.

"I went to check on Chet," I said too loudly.

"You must've run the whole way," Mama said to her reflection, "and you're not even dressed. You've missed breakfast!"

"I had cereal before."

"Then, hurry up," Mama said, turning to me. "We can walk together. Your father and Will have already gone. Mr. Early took ill, so Will is to usher in his place."

I moved to head upstairs.

She gripped my shoulder and turned me around. "Your hair is a *mess.*" She leaned down to brush the strands out of my face. "Is that a black eye?" Mama stood upright, put her gloved hands on her delicate waist. She opened her mouth to speak, paused with a frown, and simply shook her head. "Brush that rat's nest and wear a hairband. Your clothes are on your bed."

I paused at the stairs. "Can I sit in the balcony today?"

Mama took another look at me. "That's a *good* idea. Mind you, the reverend and the whole choir can see you up there. No sniggling."

"Don't wait for me. I'm right behind you."

Mama hesitated a moment, and went out.

The instant she closed the door behind her, I turned and rushed to the kitchen phone, dialing Jimmy's number from the list on the wall. I held my breath, hoping he hadn't left for church already.

"Hello?"

"Jimmy, it's me, Lucy."

"Hey, Lucy, what…"

"Meet me in the balcony at Church. I need help. Got a *big* problem."

"What sorta problem?"

"A … *gardening* problem."

A second of silence, then "I'll be there."

I hung up without saying goodbye and ran up the stairs, not caring which dress waited for me, so long as it had pockets.

In the balcony I saw the usual smattering of kids and teens on the left;

on the right, a young couple with a baby, and old Mr. Reinhart in his clean, Sunday overalls. I spotted Jimmy near the wall, at the far end of a pew, and made my way to him.

The small shelf on the back of the pew before us, above the shelf for hymnals, held cards and a single, stubby pencil with no eraser, like the ones at the bowling alley. The cards could be filled out with requested prayers and placed in the offering plates passed near the end of services. From where I sat, I couldn't see Daddy or Will, but knew they'd be standing against the back wall, right beneath us. Will—as youngest—would be the usher sent up to the balcony. On other occasions when he ushered, I'd write a "special request," like, "Please, God, make my dong bigger and heal that big-ass pimple on my butt," and sign his name to it. He'd always pluck them out, yet sometimes his lips pursed hard with the effort not to laugh. He'd be disappointed today. Soon as I sat, I took one of the pencils and wrote to Jimmy instead: *We have to go. Important. Wait for doxology.*

I could see the questions in Jimmy's eyes. He spread his hands, palms up. In answer, I wrote *Help Chet* on the card, and showed it to Jimmy.

The music director approached the pulpit and faced the choir. After a dramatic moment of silence, he raised his arms and the singers stood as one. Mrs. Cleary pounded out an introductory phrase on the organ. The congregation stood and everyone began to sing, except Jimmy and me.

"Praise God from whom all blessings flow.

Praise him all creatures here below…"

I slipped out along the wall. Jimmy sank down and slid off the pew like he'd melted. Then he crawled up the inclined floor toward me, like one of those ridiculous spies from Mad magazine.

On the stairs down, I punched him on the arm. He spread his hands again and whispered, "What? Trying to stay outta sight." I turned and continued quietly, shaking my head all the way. The door to the small brick patio beside the church had been propped open, the coast clear. The ushers hadn't come out for their smoke break yet.

"C'mon, I know a shortcut," I told Jimmy.

I headed around the corner, only to be brought up short by the sight of Annie Maude, standing quietly in the shadows, accompanied by a friendly-looking cocker spaniel.

"Fancy meeting *you* here, young lady," she said.

"Grandma!" What are you—"

"I can make a good guess as to where you two are headed," she said. "I just got fresh herbs from Ruth's garden. Do you have the juju she made?"

She saw I'd become confused. "The doll," Annie Maude said.

"Yes, here." I held my pocket open for her to see.

"Let's have it, then" she said, reaching. Her hands were stained yellow and dusted in something green.

I gingerly lifted the doll—"juju" Grandma had called it—in its cloth, my lower lip quivering, tears stinging my eyes, my thoughts on Chet. "Please don't take it away, Grandma."

"What is it?" Jimmy asked.

Annie Maude gave him a look. He backed off.

She turned to me. "I'm not here to stop you, honey. I'm here to help."

I reluctantly handed Ruth's creation over to Grandma.

Annie Maude held the juju gently between her palms, shut her eyes, and became still. The cocker spaniel whimpered, grew quiet again as Jimmy smoothed the fur on its back.

Grandma pulled the cloth away from the juju.

The doll lay in her palm, looking like it had when Ruth first made it. The herbs looked fresher, the arm seemed mended, and the wishbone had found its way back into its original position.

"B-but," I stammered.

"What *is* that?" Jimmy asked.

Nobody answered.

Grandma smiled, said, "Don't worry about that now. We can talk later." She rewrapped the juju in the cloth, and handed it to me. "You two have somewhere to be and time is short. Take it and go."

"Would you drive us?"

"No, my business here is not done. Chet's mother has it in for your Daddy, and I think she might make a scene at the Third Sunday Dinner this afternoon. I'm here to warn him so he can go smooth her feathers before that happens. But first, I've got to get his attention."

She turned to Jimmy. "Hand me that," she said, pointing to a box of dog treats hidden in the planter alongside the path.

Annie Maude removed the lone treat from the box, crouched beside the dog, and whispered in its ear. She gave the dog the treat. While it chewed, she fitted the box over its head. Surprisingly, it didn't complain, even as she guided it toward the door and into the church. We watched the dog wander toward the sanctuary, and heard the first sounds of surprise from the congregation. Daddy would be the one to take charge of getting the dog out of the church.

"Well, *that's* done," Annie Maude said. "Now, get going."

I slipped the wrapped doll carefully back into my pocket and grabbed Jimmy's arm. We headed toward the back of the church.

"Chet's house isn't too far past mine," I said.

Behind the church, where the youth team played softball, a dozen or more crows milled around. Bickering and snapping at each other, they pecked at popcorn and bits of trash left from the game the day before. Jimmy stopped short at the pitcher's mound. Puddles from yesterday's storm marked the rest of the field. One of the crows fluttered down near our feet to peck at a gum wrapper.

"Just wait a minute," he said. "What are we up to here? Was that a *voodoo* doll?"

"Not really."

"But it's witch-stuff, like in her garden, and Grandma's in on it. That's why you said you had a *gardening problem.*" Jimmy smacked his forehead. "What've you got me into, *now?*" Though he sounded worried, as a gust of wind lifted the blond curls from his forehead, I saw his eyes shone bright with excitement. Wind whipped my skirt around my legs, and I looked up to see that dark clouds had gathered again. I thought about that terrible run I'd made through the woods to Ruth's house, something I didn't want to repeat to get to Chet's.

Was that just yesterday?

"Lemme see that thing," he said, reaching.

I turned so he couldn't get to my pocket. "There's no time! We've got to get to Chet before church is over." My voice sounded high and whiny in the wind and gathering gloom. "Please, Jimmy, just trust me," I looked him straight in the eye. The crows had gone quiet. In the silence, it seemed they too, waited for his answer.

"Tell me on the way," he said. A single drop of rain spattered his cheek. Blinking, he looked up at the sky.

The crows rose noisily around us, twice as many as I'd thought. We both jumped, then cowered down, Jimmy putting his arms up to shield us.

"Shit," he said once the air cleared of birds.

A quick glance back the way we'd come assured me that our escape hadn't been noticed—there was no one in sight but for a lone crow, feet away. I shivered to see it staring at me. My hand went protectively to the doll in my pocket. When a fat raindrop hit the top of my head, I turned and ran, Jimmy following right behind me.

The rain came down in earnest.

~ ~ ~

"This is a minefield of puddles," Jimmy said, as we ran up the alley that led past my house to Chet's. Pretending the puddles were a real danger, Jimmy hopped over them, and took little dancing steps around those that were hard to avoid. Even so, he kept up with me.

"Won't be much farther," I told him. We'd slowed to a trot. We had to keep our Sunday clothes as clean as possible. Our shoes were muddied already. If we got caught, we would be in enough trouble for ditching church. No point in adding to our problems.

Before I knew why, I found myself running up my driveway.

"What are you doing?" Jimmy yelled from behind.

"Need pants and real shoes. I'll be quick." I pulled off my muddy church shoes. "Open the door for me."

He did, and I ran up to my room. I threw the shoes under my bed, and pulled out the juju and placed it on my pillow. My wet dress clung to me. I struggled to get it over my head, then scrambled into dungarees, and an old shirt. Scooping up my sneakers, I ran back down. Jimmy stood in the kitchen, dabbing his face dry with a dish towel.

"Not that it helps," Jimmy said with a sheepish look. He seemed to consider something, then said, "Hey, I thought Will was at church."

"He is."

"Who was looking out your bedroom window when we came up?"

"No one. Will *is* at church. Helen's at Jackie's house. There's no one here."

"I could have sworn I saw someone."

Penny?

"We don't have time for Scare-a-boo," I said, "if that's what you're up to." He shrugged.

I plucked my raincoat off the hook on the porch and held it out to Jimmy. He looked blankly at me. I shook it at him "Put it on," I commanded.

He looked at the coat in horror. "No way I'm wearing kittens! Besides, I'm already wet."

"Your Mama will be even madder if you're dirty too."

"She'll be madder anyway."

"I'm looking at those itty-bitty boy titties through your shirt, right now. You know what's worse than a hurricane, don't you?"

He snatched the coat from me to protect his chest, and grudgingly shrugged it on.

The sleeves were a couple of inches too short, and I had to bite the inside of my lip to keep from smiling.

"A'right. Let's go a'ready," he said. I followed him out, gripping the wrapped doll against my chest. We dashed down the alley.

At Chet's house, in the gloom, we crouched behind the hedge between the alley and his back yard. Peering through the wet leaves, I could see a light on in Chet's bedroom. The car sat crooked in the driveway, and we heard angry voices from inside the house—probably the Boyds, fighting.

"That his room?" Jimmy whispered, from behind. His narrowed eyes went from the kitchen, where the voices came from, to Chet's lighted upstairs window at the opposite end of the house.

I nodded, glad to see the sash partly opened.

Jimmy's fingers massaged his chin and his brow furrowed. I avoided looking at the kittens on the hood framing his face, afraid of laughing in the middle of his transformation.

Within moments, Jimmy had become that special soldier/secret agent I'd seen him turn into on numerous occasions, like he had back at the church or any time we competed in play.

He snapped into action, pointing to himself, then to me, and following that with the finger-walk motion. Backing away, he jerked a thumb toward the alley behind us, and stood. I followed.

"Act natural and do exactly what I do," he said, his natural walk anything but. We sauntered to one corner of the yard and beyond until we were out of sight of Chet's house.

Jimmy motioned for us to crouch below the level of the hedge, and said, "Now that they think the strangers have gone on by, we'll double back. Do what I do." He began waddle-walking in a crouch toward the corner we'd just left. Following, I bit my tongue and hoped he had a plan. Somewhere along the way, the rain slackened and quit. The trees continued to drip on us.

Reaching the corner, Jimmy took off the raincoat and handed it to me. He pried a hole through the hedge, close to the ground where he found a separation between shrubs large enough for us to pass through. "Lie down in there and look into the yard while I tell you what I think we should do."

I put on the raincoat, placed the juju in the pocket, and did like he asked, getting a fairly good look across Chet's back yard from a worm's-eye-view.

"You see the brick barbecue, the birdbath, and the little shed?" he said. "We'll use those for cover as we make for our target, the trellis running up the house beside Chet's bedroom window. Once we're up against the house, no one can see us unless they're in the back yard."

"Copy that, Agent Kittens," I said.

He ignored my dig.

"I'll move to the barbecue and wait for you there. If someone comes out back while you're moving, drop to the ground quick and make yourself flat as you can. Shouldn't be too hard, he said with a glance at my chest."

I pulled myself out of the hedge and punched him again.

"I wish we had camouflage fatigues to help us hide better. And since I'm wishing for stuff—if you're going to keep hitting me, I should have a flak jacket."

I didn't bother to ask.

On his stomach, Jimmy wriggled through the hedge, got to his knees, and dashed to the shadows behind the barbecue. Following, one of my braids caught in the hedge, and I lost a shoe. I got my hair free, but twigs had tangled in the braid.

Jimmy saw me struggling to free my shoe, and mouthed silently, "leave it."

No way. I wasn't going up that trellis without my left shoe. I got it free, and ran to him.

"You're such a spaz" he said, sounding a lot like Will.

Without thinking about how he might cry out, I punched him in the shoulder harder than I ever had. His eyes got big and he made a silent "screaming" face.

"You're going to ruin everything if you make me break noise discipline!" he whispered.

Again, I didn't ask.

"I'll run to the birdbath, and signal. Then you head for it. Then, I'll make for the shed and you'll follow. *Then*, we're home free 'cause the trellis is right there."

Agent Kittens really enjoyed giving me orders! He was eating this up.

We got to the trellis without disaster.

Testing the slats of the structure fixed to the house, Jimmy said. "It feels strong enough."

"I know it is. That's how Chet sneaks out."

He went first and got to the window quickly. Once he'd climbed in, I started up more slowly, worried about the juju dropping out of my raincoat pocket. I brushed aside the wisteria creepers and a couple of daddy long-legs that got in my face. Crawling in over the sill, I saw Chet sleeping and Jimmy moving silently through the room, checking out the monster models, the little league softball trophy, and the glittering collection of crystals and polished stones. Chet looked small, curled up under his blanket in bed. Standing over him, I pulled out the juju. I opened the cloth wrapping and held the thing close in the dim light to get a better look—still good as new.

Penny appeared.

She snapped her fingers at the ends of my pigtails. "Scare-a-boo, got you," she whispered.

My hair caught fire.

She giggled.

I dropped the juju. Panicking, I slapped at my hair with my raincoat sleeves, and turned toward Jimmy. He had his shirt off in an instant, and smothered me and the flames with it. I choked on the stink of burnt hair, struggled to cough quietly.

Worried we might step on the juju, I looked down, didn't see it. Penny had disappeared too.

"Who…I-I mean, what was *that*?" Jimmy stammered.

I dropped to the floor to see if we'd kicked it under the bed.

Pale spiders—Penny's hands—held the juju directly under the center of the bed.

She gave me a smile, all gums and baby teeth, and gently set the magic doll down.

"Penny," I coughed out, shaken.

"Who?" Jimmy asked, and then he lay beside me on his stomach, looking under the bed too late to see Penny. She had vanished like the smoke from my burnt hair.

"Who said, 'Scare-a-boo'?" he demanded. "How did your hair catch fire? What—"

Chet moaned and shifted in the bed above.

I backed away, crouching. As Jimmy backed out, I motioned for him to stay low and quiet. He took his shirt off my shoulders. Turning up his nose at the smell, he pulled it on.

Chet had become still again. He farted in his sleep, and Jimmy giggled.

"It's working already," he said, pinching his nose. "Let's get outta here."

I felt relieved, and also had the same sort of gratitude I'd had toward Penny the time she'd returned my lucky penny, so long ago.

But boy, what a fright!

~ ~ ~

When we got back to the Church, there was still plenty to eat. I had changed back into my dress. Jimmy would have some explaining to do later for the sorry state of his clothes and for smelling of burnt hair. Even so, he was all smiles. "Mission accomplished," he whispered to me once we'd arrived, and then again later around a mouth full of Aunt Aldean's macaroni and cheese.

I tried to give him the smile I knew he wanted.

"Who's Penny?" he whispered.

I put down my cornbread, took a drink of tea and wiped my mouth to give me time to think. "I don't know, but I bet she's some of Grandma's doings."

"How do you know her name?"

I gave him the truth. "That's just what I call her."

"She a ghost?"

I shrugged. "Ask Grandma."

He nodded uncertainly. I knew he would not question her about Penny, because he'd always been a bit afraid of Annie Maude.

Chet's mother arrived late, Daddy with her. He carried a big chocolate cake. They both smiled.

After greetings, Mrs. Boyd made an announcement. "*Blessings* to you all for praying for my boy," she said, beaming. "The LORD has *heard* you and by HIS loving grace, HE has *healed* my son. The fever has *broken*. *Praise* the LORD." She raised her arms and beaming face toward the heavens.

"She ain't looked under the bed, I guess," Jimmy said with a crooked smile.

"Yet," I said.

"Should we scoot over there and get that doll back before she does?"

"Nope. Doesn't matter. I got this chicken to eat, and then I'm gonna have some of that chocolate cake.

Slow Debbie and The Lunch Lady
1968

The first time I saw the girl, the word "Angel" leapt to mind. She had short hair, so light the blond strands looked silver. Her eyes were lavender-colored, with mere suggestions of lashes and brows against her ghostly skin.

On the sidewalk out front, wide eyed, I watched as her family moved into the house next door. I jumped when Mama grabbed my arm. She tugged me away, saying, "Stop standing in the rain like an idiot." Inside, I went straight to a window that gave a view of their porch. I dragged up a chair and planted my elbows on the sill. Spotting a monkey, carried in a large, ornate cage, I gasped aloud and pressed my forehead against the glass until the animal disappeared into the house. I didn't want to miss a single second of that procession of exotic looking people and their colorful belongings.

The rest of the family—parents, and an older brother and a sister, who might have been twins—all had darker skin and dark hair. The father rolled up his sleeves, revealing tattoos on his forearms. The mother had her hair pulled back, secured by something that sparkled as she moved. But the pale girl drew my eyes most. She stood taller than me and might have been older.

Unexpectedly, she looked up and waved, smiling widely. I grinned and waved back before she, too, disappeared inside. I wondered what grade she would be in, what games she played, and if she'd be nice. Would she like me? Did she have the same big set of crayons I did?

~ ~ ~

The next day, I fidgeted in class, watching the clock for lunchtime, when mixed grades would file into the big lunchroom to eat together. Sliding my tray down the counter, I hardly noticed what got plopped into each section. I kept craning my neck to survey the room for that pale hair, which should have been easy to spot.

"They're not here," the Lunch Lady said. I whipped around in surprise.

She'd never spoken to me before. She looked right at me, and my stomach lurched.

"Oh," I said, too afraid to say more.

I had been terrified of the lunch lady since first grade. Her face, a chiseled monument to discipline, showed little emotion. I couldn't remember a single day she hadn't been there at her post, commanding her "all-colored" staff, who were obviously afraid of her too. Stories went around, something to do with a husband disappearing without a trace some years earlier. Her hair, under its delicate net, kept its snooty coif. She drove a Cadillac convertible, long and green, with white insides. In it, she'd roll down the street slowly, wearing gloves, a scarf over her hair and big, cat-eye sunglasses. Her toy poodle sat regally in the passenger seat. I always stopped to watch when she went by. All us kids did. Once I saw her in the bank, with the dog cradled on her arm like a clutch.

The teller's over bright smile said it all: The Lunch Lady was not one of us.

Her home wasn't far from my own, up a climbing, curved road, too steep for bikes. The place stood at the end of a long drive lined with trees, looking like a castle, with a lush lawn of imported grass flanked by walls of tall, evergreen shrubs. On the other side of the road, you could walk down a slight slope from the shoulder to find a spot overlooking the town. I'd hiked up there with friends once. We'd thought maybe the Lunch Lady occasionally watched us from that lookout.

"They both went *home* for lunch," she announced with disapproval. "Not the other one—she *won't* be attending Byrd Elementary."

How did she know who I was looking for? Had she watched from her lookout as they moved in and saw me watching too?

Yet, too afraid to ask, I felt relief when the Lunch Lady turned to the next kid in line. I shuffled along, blinking and puzzled.

The other one? Of course, she meant the beautiful, pale girl.

That evening, Will told me the kids called her Slow Debbie. He'd learned this from her older brother, also in sixth grade. He followed that with a casual remark, cold in the way he tossed it off: "She's not right."

The weeks went by, the weather warmed, and the days lengthened. I joined Slow Debbie on the long L-shaped porch. Turned out, she *did* have a complete set of 64 crayons, with built-in sharpener, and a shoebox of nubs and pieces. I brought my set too and a stack of coloring books. Hunched over our work, a comfort grew between us.

I took Chet to meet Slow Debbie, but he seemed uncomfortable around her. Had he heard she wasn't *right*? I didn't ask. Since she wasn't allowed beyond her yard without one of her family, she could not join us on our usual adventures at the river. I liked having her all to myself anyway, and made time for her when I wasn't hanging out with Chet.

As the plums ripened on the trees, the porch at her house became ours. On wash days, we had crisp scents of bluing and starch, on others, the aroma of spiced dishes simmering. On blustery days, we had to hold our papers down, and on bright days, we kept in the shade since the sun burned her skin quickly. My favorites were the rainy ones. Being curtained off from the outside world gave the porch a cozy feeling.

Our conversations at times turned disjointed and spontaneous. She taught me the game of repeating words until they seemed to make no sense.

"Of, of, of, of, of, of, of, of, of, of, of, of, of, of, of, of," Deb said. "What does that mean?"

"I don't know anymore," I giggled.

"How do you spell 'of'" she asked.

Sounding it out in my head, I said, "o-v."

We laughed because that's the way the word sounded like it should be spelled. I'd never noticed until then.

"Basket, basket, basket, elastic, Alaska, how do you spell 'basket'" she asked.

I shrugged, "I d'know, Idaho, I'll ask it!"

That game and the occasional rhyming bits rolled us to our backs, laughing. I understood now what my brother meant by "not right," and why the kids called her Slow Debbie. She had an odd sense of things, yet most of the time, I enjoyed following her down the strange pathways of her thinking. To me, she was something pure, somehow beyond the rest of us. I began to call her Deb. If she ever said my name, I don't remember.

Occasionally, her mother, Lally, would look out at us through the screen door. She sometimes set out a tray of cookies and Kool-Aid. She said little, nodded to us, her smile kind and genuine. Finally, on a mild Tuesday afternoon, she moved the monkey's cage outside, commenting that their family had never lived in such a warm place. Her voice, with a strange accent, sounded musical and lilting. She wore bracelets with little bells that jingled softly.

"He's a squirrel monkey," Lally said. "His name is Mister Charlie."

Looking into the monkey's bright eyes and listening to his excited chattering, I was beside myself with delight. The red fez on his head had a little yellow tassel that matched the piping on his maroon vest.

Lisa Snellings & Alan M. Clark

"Very pleased to meet you," I said. As I put a finger through the bars, he grasped it gently, sort of like a handshake. Just like that, he became an equal, almost human. I'd crossed a delicate line.

After that, the porch belonged to him too. We'd hold up our work for his approval. Some days, I'd back up near the cage so he could tug on my ponytail. He'd work at the ribbon until he got it loose, and my hair fell all around me. I liked the way that felt, and it made Deb giggle. When he fell asleep in the sun, we'd sit and watch him, sometimes holding hands.

July came, humid and hot. I spent less time on my bike and with Chet, and more with Deb. We had moved on to paper dolls, a gift from Annie Maude. We took to setting them up and inventing little stories about them. Well, mostly I set them up and Deb blew them down, raising her arms in delight.

At home, I made paper dolls of Deb, me, and Mr. Charlie. The next day, I set them up on the Varma's porch, then knocked on the door. When Deb came out and saw them, she squealed and clapped her hands. "That's us," she said, giggling, "and Mr. Charlie too!"

Taking another look, I realized I'd made a good likeness of all three of us. After that, I got my first sketch book and began to draw regularly.

One humid, cloudy afternoon, we ventured out into the yard in search of cooler spots to play. Though the pecans were still fuzzy and green, the plums had fully ripened. Zinnias and black-eyed Susans had bloomed. An old, towering magnolia guarded one corner of the yard, the shady space underneath inviting us in. We settled down inside the hollow formed of waxy leaves, and shortly, noticed a soft mewing. Crawling carefully toward the sound, we discovered a cat with four kittens. Their eyes had opened, and they rolled and played around their sleeping mother. She opened her eyes to watch us, but didn't hiss or move. We sat still, and, eventually, one of the kittens wandered over to us. Deb scooped the creature up gently, turning it this way and that. Holding the kitten in one hand, she turned its face away and touched its tiny butthole. She held the fuzzy animal toward me. The kitten's legs wriggled frantically as I touched the same spot she had. An unexpected sort of thrill filled me and with it, an odd discomfort. I pulled my hand back and looked at it. I didn't want to play with the kittens anymore. I got up, wiped my hands vigorously on my shorts, and went in search of plums. Deb joined me beside the porch. While the purple fruit had become juicy and sweet, I missed the yellow ones and their tartness.

A light sprinkling grew to a steady drizzle. Deb put a plum in her pocket for Mister Charlie, and a handful of little green pea pods. They couldn't have

70

been the same type of peas that came from a store, unless they were babies. I thought to get a bright Zinnia for Mister Charlie's fez, then remembered he'd been without his clothes through the recent hot days. Instead, I pinched off some of the pink blossoms to help decorate his cage.

That night, as usual, I lay in bed in my second-floor room and listened for the approach of Penny's ghost. I didn't look forward to a visit, yet the habit of listening for her couldn't be undone. Though I say "listening," that's not exactly right. Sometimes, I could *feel* her approach before I saw her.

The house remained quiet. With the windows open to the cool air, I heard dogs barking, a distant siren, and the wind ruffling leaves in the trees. I might have begun to doze off when I heard voices outside. One of them belonged to Deb's father, Mr. Varma. I couldn't make out his words. Clear from his tone, he'd grown upset. Quietly, I got up and went to the bathroom, where the window gave a view of their house. Mr. Varma stood at the bottom of the porch steps. Seeing a bald spot on top of his head surprised me. I'd never noticed that before. Because he stood shirtless, I discovered his tattoos ran up to his shoulders and down his back. Then I saw Mister Charlie in his hands. Limp and motionless, his little arms and legs hung loosely, like a terrible doll—a Mister Charlie doll. Lally stood on the porch above him, her hands over her face. Mr. Varma walked out of sight around the side of the house. Lally turned slowly and went back inside. I don't know how long I stood there, or what I hoped for.

Back in my bed, lying with eyes wide open, breath hitched in my throat. *Mister Charlie is dead.* I didn't think I'd sleep, but I did.

~ ~ ~

The next morning, the smell of laundry reached me before I heard the washing machine. Ruth had arrived.

Memory of the night before fell on me suddenly. A few weighted minutes passed before I turned to face a day in which I'd find out about Mister Charlie.

Downstairs, breakfast waited on a plate covered by another, upside-down plate. Still in my pajamas, I sat to eat.

Mama breezed in. "Eat up and get dressed. It's grocery day."

I loved grocery day, yet wanted to stay where I might settle the hard ball of unease in my chest. I had hope that I'd dreamed what happened to Mister Charlie. Going with Mama, I had to carry my troubles with me.

"Why do you do that?" I asked as Mama let off the gas halfway down the block.

"Do what?"

"You speed up, then coast, then speed up, then coast, over and over."

"I save gas that way," Mama said, stupidly.

"Will says it's dumb to think that. He doesn't like you doing it, either. He says accelerating uses more gas than keeping your speed even."

"Is *Will* driving this car?"

"*Noooo!*"

She reached over and turned on the radio, no doubt to drown me out.

I noticed we were going a different way. "Did you forget about Grandma?"

"Of course not. Grandma had someone to see."

"Why do you have to listen to that *country crap*?"

"Language, Lucy."

"That doesn't answer my question."

Mama pinched her lips tightly.

"Turn off your blinker," I said. "You never do."

"The turn-off is broken. I forget!" She glared at me in the rearview mirror.

And so went my carping, the whole trip.

Once we'd returned from shopping, I couldn't wait to change into shorts and go next door.

Deb sat quietly on the steps, and the squirrel monkey sat in his cage.

"Mister Charlie!" I cried, dashing onto porch and dropping to my knees before him. "You're alive!"

How could that be possible? The vision of him lying limp, Mr. Varma's unexpected bald spot, his muscular back covered in tattoos—what the hell? A terrible dream, then?

The little monkey chattered and choffed angrily at me. He wore the fez and vest, yet the small hat sat low, nearly to his little brows, and he shook it off. His eyes looked wide and hard. He didn't seem happy to see me. I turned around to see if he'd reach for my hair. He didn't touch it. Instead, he pushed to the back of the cage and sat hunched over, head down. I joined Deb on the steps. When she didn't look up, I took her hand. Finally, she looked me in the eyes for a long moment. I expected her to say something, but she returned to staring at her feet.

Lally opened the door. "Pet," she said.

Deb got up and walked into the house.

I sat there for a moment, clutching the paper doll books, and took a long look at Mister Charlie. Still at the back of his cage, he pulled and bit at the piping on the little vest. He glanced around, not at me. Mister Charlie wasn't himself. I stood and went home.

That evening, Mama said, "Lally says Debbie isn't feeling well. She's to stay inside until she gets better. You shouldn't visit until you see her outside again."

~ ~ ~

The days went by. I rode my bike, caught up with other friends, went fishing with Dad.

One afternoon, as she folded linens, Ruth said, "I'm sorry your friend can't play with you. She ain't right, yet in a good way."

Did she see what I saw? I don't know why I couldn't ask her that.

~ ~ ~

We traveled to my Great Uncle Samuel Higginbotham's big house in Georgia for a family reunion that lasted all weekend. While there, I didn't think much about ghosts, Deb, or Mister Charlie. Apparently, I had cousins everywhere and, it seemed, most had come to the reunion. We had tables loaded with delicious foods, galvanized tubs full of iced sodas, games on the lawn, and fireworks. We even took a sneak-trip to the Higginbotham funeral home. No bodies there. The coffins were cool to the touch, with fancy insides. I thought of the lunch lady's car.

By the time we got home, August had come, bringing the worst muggy heat. Worn out from all the sun and travel, I sat on my bed and let myself fall back, grateful for the familiar mattress. I lay there, still in my shoes, arms out, eyes closed, trying not to not think of anything as dusk fell outside and my room darkened.

I tried to ignore the *plink* at my window, but there came another, followed by the unmistakable sound of a handful of pebbles striking the glass. I got up to look outside. The streetlights had begun to sputter on. In the side yard, I saw Deb; so pale in the darkness, and shockingly naked. In a panic, I cast about for anything—my sheets, my unpacked suitcase. My clothes were too small. Without thinking, I plucked one of Mama's nightgowns from the laundry basket in the hall, rolling it into a ball as I went down the stairs. I slowed my pace, trying not to draw my parents' attention; Dad on the front porch with a cigarette, Mama in the kitchen making sandwiches. The smell of coffee and music from a radio drifted through the house. Mama and Daddy tended to late hours on vacations, and though home, they hadn't shaken the habit yet. Muttering something about having left stuff in the car, I went outside. I dashed to the side yard and found Deb spinning, arms in the air. Two long, dark scars ran down her back. Seeing them gave me pause. What had happened to her, I wondered.

Struggling awkwardly with the material, I managed to get the nightgown over her head, and her arms in the sleeves. I couldn't get the buttons done up because she wouldn't stand still. She looked down at the billowy white cotton and grinned, then took off like a shot toward the street. I ran after her, and nearly caught up as she turned off onto the road leading up to the lunch lady's house. In an urgent, raspy whisper. I called out, "Stop! Wait!" I'd never seen her run more than a few yards and had no idea she could move so fast. Up the hill we went, Deb fleet and graceful, me huffing along in flip flops, my throat beginning to burn. Fearing for her safety pushed me. She stopped at the look-out, right across from the Lunch Lady's house, and turned around to wait for me. The moon, full and glorious, hung like a beacon over the miniature town below. I'd never been up there at night.

I struggled to catch my breath. Deb looked at me with what appeared to be amusement, took my shoulders, and turned me toward my left. Across the road, a sea of moving, blinking lights spread out before us. My mouth dropped open.

Lightning bugs!

I'd never seen them like that, and in such numbers, like they'd gathered for some purpose. Their lights went on and on, a river flowing through the trees and past the shrubs, into the distance. Without warning, Deb ran into the stream of yellow-green lights, as if dashing into the surf on a best-ever beach day. She raised her arms and twirled, half dancing, the light picking out folds of the nightgown, and pale strands of her hair. I chased after her, my fear of being discovered keeping me hunkered down.

Past the line of trees, Deb veered right, and plopped down on the grass. The lightning bugs around her scattered. She fell back to lie in the grass, moved her arms and legs together in arcs, like jumping jacks. Though I hadn't grown up with much snow, I knew how to make snow angels. Joining in, we made grass angels together.

My arms began to tire and my breathing came in hard gasps from all the running. When I stopped moving, so did she. The lightning bugs closed in. We lay there, on the softest, finest grass I'd ever felt, watching them fly and flash their little lights. I had an impression of being underwater and looking up at a surface twinkling in sunlight.

I must be dreaming, I thought, *still lying on my bed in my clothes.* I rolled my head toward Deb, watched the lights caught in her eyes. She had also captured me—I saw myself in those lavender-colored eyes.

I wondered if anyone would find our grass angels the next day, and whether they'd know that at least one of them was real.

Deb's head jerked back violently. Her chin pointed skyward, her eyes staring. At once, the lightning bugs seemed to vanish. Lights out.

Blinking the afterlights away, I followed Deb's gaze to the Lunch Lady's house, to the roof. I made out a shape crouched beside the chimney: Penny, in her little sack of a gown. Even in silhouette, I knew the ghost. My blood turned to ice.

In a seamless movement, Deb rolled over and got to her feet. Penny also stood.

They appeared to look directly at one another. Deb began to mumble something under her breath, and her fingers twitched. I didn't know if the words had meaning, or if her fingers were tracing some pattern. I stared wide-eyed at her. When I looked back toward the roof, Penny had vanished.

I found Deb looking at me, her face calm, her gaze even. I had an impression that she held deep wisdom and a strength that I'd known nothing about, that perhaps no other person knew about. That moment, she had the appearance of a statue, a saint masterfully carved from purest white marble, a presence eternal, yet unreachable.

Then she put her hands over her mouth, giggled, and took off toward the rear yard of the lunch Lady's house.

Oh, no!

I struggled to keep up, afraid to call out. Deb disappeared into the darkness where the trees grew thicker, blocking the moonlight. She reappeared, still running.

I tripped over something, banging my shin hard. Even as I stumbled and clapped my hands over my mouth, a yelp escaped me.

Deb stopped and did the same, in a pure mimic that brought me a flash of Mister Charlie.

Terrified I'd awakened the lunch lady or her dog, I crouched, not moving a muscle. I rubbed my hand over my shin, felt a lump forming. Mama would want to know how I got hurt. How would I explain it away? The bruise ached fiercely.

I felt around to see what I'd tripped over, and found a garden stone carved with letters that spelled "Tiffy."

The dog! When had I last seen the little poodle?

The shift to night complete, near full dark came with clouds hiding the moon. Adjusting to the dimness, I spotted another stone, and another. I crawled forward on my hands and knees. They all bore the name, Tiffy. And there were more—at least three, before shadows swallowed them—each one like the others. I thought back on all the times I'd seen the little poodle riding in the lunch lady's car, the wind ruffling its curls, its little, pink tongue peeking out.

Their little, pink *tongues*. The thought stunned me.

Lights snapped on. I heard a clattering, saw a door of the house flung wide. Golden light escaped, finding us both. The lunch lady emerged, barreling toward us, shouting.

Angry, tall, and terrifying, she carried something long that glinted as she closed the distance between us.

"I see you!" she roared, her hair flying loose, long, and wild. She'd become the witch from every scary story. "I've called your house! I'm calling the police after I shoot you both!"

Squinting against the light, I could make out her bare feet, and the shotgun.

"Run!" I cried.

I couldn't see a thing with the moon now totally obscured by clouds, but had a rough sense of where we had to go. Leading the way, running at full speed, I avoided the thickets of shrubs and trees.

The sound of the shotgun blast clapped against our ears, reverberating across the distance. Having fled the more lighted area near the house, I quickly lost my way in the pitch-blackness, not knowing how far I had run.

Suddenly, running too fast, we hit the pavement of the narrow road. I tried to turn to avoid a tumble downhill off the steep edge of the lane. I stumbled, Deb grabbed me, and we fell over the edge together. Rolling into the gully, formed at the steep side of the hill, we came to a jarring stop against something hard, the breath knocked from us both. Once I could think again, I realized with relief that the Lunch Lady had not followed. I heard a little dog barking in the distance.

Tiffy?

The moon emerged from behind the clouds.

The backs of my legs ached. My thighs and calves had scratches, some deep enough to draw blood. I burned inside and my skin stung all over.

We untangled ourselves.

Deb's marks appeared much worse. She'd wrapped herself around me as we'd fallen, pinning my arms under hers. Mama's gown had been torn in several places. Deb had scrapes and cuts that looked painful, and a dark spot across her nose.

A flash of headlights played over the roadside brush above us. Car doors slammed, and voices approached the drop off. The police flashlight beams found us.

~ ~ ~

I got the worst whipping of my life, and a grounding, and so missed the last week of freedom before school started. Mama and Daddy even took my books. No longer would I be allowed to play with Deb. Or she with me. "Ever," Mama had said. *Ever.*

After school, each day, I'd see her out on her porch, coloring. For a little while, she wore a sling on her left arm.

Every day, I stood at a window that faced their house, watching, a wave held ready. Sometimes Deb waved back. Sometimes she didn't. Most of the time, she didn't even look up. I tried, but couldn't see the corner where Mister Charlie's cage would have been.

On a rainy September day, the leaves beginning to fall from the trees, I arrived home from school to find the Varma's had gone. Just gone.

"They packed up and left this morning," Mama said.

I lay face down on my bed, holding back tears.

When my grounding ended on October 4th, the day before my 10th birthday, I walked over to look at the house where they had lived. All the magic had gone with the Varma family, *vanished.* I wandered their empty back yard a few times, looking for anything Deb might have left behind. The magnolia blossoms lay curled and brown around the tree—no sign of the cat and her kittens. I cupped my hands and peered into the windows of the house, saw empty walls and floors. Without the lush ferns, and fan-backed wicker, the house looked worn and ordinary, like ours. I didn't find so much as a crayon mark on the porch.

Heading back toward my house, I found a twist of yellow threads at the border of the two properties—a string from Mister Charlie's fez, I decided. The following weekend, still hurting from a sense of loss with the Varma family's departure, I made a choice that, at the time, made me uneasy. I dropped the yellow string into one of the milky white jars from my red cabinet in Grandma's cellar. Before doing that, I consulted with Annie Maude, telling her that I only wanted relief from my sadness over the loss of Mister Charlie, and my longing to be with the angel again, yet didn't want to forget anything else about my experience with Slow Deb.

"Such a 'proviso' sometimes works," Grandma said, "if it isn't too complicated and you speak it aloud before placing the object in the jar."

A few weeks later, a couple without children moved into the empty house. They put a pair of no-nonsense rocking chairs on the porch, a simple table between.

~ ~ ~

That winter, I had pneumonia. I spent an agonizing two weeks in the hospital, stayed in bed at home for over a month under an oxygen tent, and didn't attend school for another month. I had fevers and fever dreams of Mister Charlie calling for my help, and me unable to find him. For the longest time, I remained too weak even to wander the house. With my world limited to inside the tent for such a long while, and everything seen through the plastic out of focus, what lay beyond began to seem imaginary. My ears roared, drowning out the nighttime creaking and sighs of our house. Maybe Penny had gone too.

I played with a hand puppet brought home from the hospital. I read the entire Happy Hollisters collection and whatever else Daddy brought home from the library. Some were science fiction books I'd already read, but I didn't mind. Sometimes, I awoke to find him sitting quietly by my bed. By the time I started eating at our kitchen table, watching television, and moving about, the world seemed much like it had before I'd left.

A long, thick braid of hair, tied with a ribbon, lay coiled on my dresser like a pale snake. My lucky penny rested in its center. My shorter hair had come in darker, with all those summers cut away, and I now wore eyeglasses—thick lenses in black frames. Returning to school, I could tell some of the kids didn't recognize me. Surprised me to find I kind of liked that. For a little while, I could be someone else, free of me. When I went through the lunch line, I couldn't tell if the lunch lady knew me. Though I didn't believe she could be fooled, no way could I tell for sure.

If she'd be willing to pretend, I would too.

~ ~ ~

Now, years later, Deb remains a persistent presence in my thoughts, along with some unavoidable regret and shame. Did we do something that killed Mr. Charlie? Did the Varmas take her away because of me? Perhaps I'll never know.

As always, I wonder if she still exists out there, somewhere. I wonder if others get to see her pale purple eyes all lit up in that smile of hers, and if that claims their hearts too. I wonder if she ever escaped her cocoon.

Does she remember me?

My wish is that she does.

My hope is that she doesn't.

Will's Way
1968

My brother's bedroom, the largest in the house, could be found down a short hallway from the living room, somewhat isolated from the rest of the house. Will had once shared the room with my older sister. Though she'd gone off to nursing school, the space remained partitioned by a wall of bookcases that reached the ceiling. Every shelf was filled, crammed with a disarray of books—many stacked on their sides with papers sticking out of them—and a large assortment of toys, laboratory items, and unidentifiable gadgets that could have been either. Chalkboards, charts, and a bounty of note cards stuck on with thumbtacks covered the backs of the bookcases. Whenever the air moved, they fluttered like moths. Jumbled as the room looked, a certain sense of order prevailed. My brother was *some kind of genius*, folks thought, so Mama and Daddy left him to himself, and he'd brag about the money they'd fork over anytime he needed "science stuff." A teacher had sent him home with an old tank of a microscope, dissecting trays, knives, and other items that had been replaced at the school with newer ones, compliments of the company that owned the cotton mill.

He'd rarely shown any interest in me—I didn't much like him either—but his room was a wonder, and most seriously off-limits.

Many a time, when he was away, I'd stand in the hall, staring at the locked door to his room, mulling over other ways I might sneak in. One time, I'd tried to get in through the trapdoor in the ceiling of his closet. I'd gone up to the attic through the main pull-down, and accidentally put my foot through the hall ceiling plaster while trying to crawl toward his room. I got in deep crap for that—grounded for a week and having to shell two bushels of peas by myself for my mother's canning. My thumbs hurt for days.

Once in a blue moon, Will would need a second pair of hands or eyes and I'd be invited in. Mostly he let me enter only if I brought him a big beetle, a lizard, or some other creature I'd caught in my "catching" jar. I'd got pretty good at sneaking up on things.

On the first day of winter break, with the cold rain coming down outside, there were few critters to hunt. By late afternoon, I'd become bored. Mama and Daddy went out that evening. The rain continued. I found nothing entertaining on television.

Will, in his room, had made little noise. I couldn't help wondering what he was up to.

I remembered the paper mâché frog I'd been working on, and decided that if I found a way to science it up, it could be the price of admission to his room. The encyclopedia had film overlays of frog innards. Using that as a guide, I cut a door in the paper mâché frog's chest and installed organs I'd fashioned from small wads of toilet paper, starch, and paint.

When it had dried, I took the frog with me and knocked on the door to Will's odd sanctuary.

"What?" he said, "I'm busy, shithead."

"Caught something for you."

With little delay, the door opened and he stuck his head out.

I held up my creation. "I made this for you."

"Yeah, that's nice. Now bug off." He started to shut the door.

"Wait. Look." I flipped the frog over and opened its chest.

He opened the door wider and leaned in for a closer look. "Huh, you made that?"

"Yep, for you." I beamed at him.

"Thanks, that's actually kind of cool."

He opened the door—success!

"Come in," he said. "I have something I can show you. Help me with this." Will gestured to his varnished microscope box.

I reached to move the chest beside it. Will stopped me, placing a hand on my arm. "Don't touch that one. It's my daddy's stuff."

"Why is his stuff in your room?"

"Not *him*, my *real* daddy."

"Oh," I said, awkwardly. "Can I see?"

"No."

Once we had the microscope box out, he opened it slowly, carefully, twisted the clips aside, then looked at me sternly and said, "Careful, now. You hold the box steady while I lift it out." He did so with reverence, and placed the microscope on the desk. The complicated device looked heavy.

"Hand me the first slide," he said, gesturing to a case of them at the far end of his desk. His words were packed with urgency and impatience.

I lifted the little glass rectangle and handed it to him carefully, not wanting to mess up and give him a reason to send me out.

He placed it on the microscope's stage. "Excellent," he said, peering into the eyepiece. I sat on the wooden box, and ran a finger around letters stamped into a metal tag on top, "OLYMPUS," they spelled.

"What do you see?" I asked him.

"Planaria," he said, "*two* headed."

"Planaria sounded like a disease to me. "Is it a germ?"

"No, stupid, it's a worm."

Even better! I stood up. "Can I see?"

"Okay. Make sure you don't touch anything. Squeeze one eye shut and look through here," he pointed at the eyepiece.

"I'm not a total dope."

"Yes, you are, and you need to take your glasses off."

I did as he asked and saw little. "It's all blurry."

"Okay," he said, "use this knob—the smaller one—and turn it just a tad while you're looking."

A few tries and I found the sharp edges of the round, lit image. The worm also popped into focus. I laughed out loud—the creature had two, arrow-shaped, cross-eyed heads.

"*I* gave it two heads," my brother said, crossing his arms and lifting his chin.

"Wow, that's crazy!" His smile told me he felt proud and wanted—no, *needed*—to show someone. I got to be the *one*. Thankfully, the cold rain kept his friends in their own houses that evening, likely not doing anything so exciting. I thought of Chet. He'd sure get a kick out of seeing the two-headed planaria. Though I felt the urge to show others what my genius brother had done, that didn't last because I liked being the *one*. I wanted to hang onto that little bit of status for as long as I could.

"But…*how*?" I asked.

"It's an experiment. Look." He handed me a single sheet of paper. He'd covered the entire page with cellophane tape, making it look waxy. The drawings of the Planaria looked even more comical than the real thing. I laughed again. Beside the drawings were step-by-step instructions for precisely slicing the worms with a scalpel so that they would grow extra heads, or tails. Also, the instructions showed how one worm might be cut in halves that would then grow into whole worms. I was *gobsmacked*.

"I'm gobsmacked," I said aloud. I'd been trying out the word—newly acquired from England—at every opportunity. This time, it actually felt appropriate. Will smiled again, and I felt quite sophisticated.

"I used my Christmas money," he said. "There's this place where I can send away for experiments, and supplies. There's even a number to call if I have questions. It's long-distance, though."

"Does it hurt them?" I asked. I usually didn't think about the feelings of bugs and other lower forms of life, but the Planaria looked kind of cute... sort of.

"Nah," Will said. He grinned, sat up straight, and squared his shoulders. "The Planaria flatworm is a simple organism. Those marks are not actual eyes." He spoke with exaggerated formality, sounding like a *real* scientist. His impish grin returned. "But isn't it neat that they can be cut in half and still live?"

I bent over to peer through the lens at the tiny creatures I'd never known existed.

"Does this work with anything else?" I didn't like the thoughts that trailed after that.

"Sure. Lots of things: lizards, spiders, tadpoles. Nothing that I could get specimens of. Anyway, bigger stuff stinks, especially dead stuff, and Ruth wouldn't have it." He removed the slide from the clips on the microscope's stage. "Put this one back and hand me the next slide in line."

I sat back down on the fancy box, carefully replaced the slide, and picked up the next one. Will slid the glass under the clips and began twisting the knob to refocus.

He chuckled. "Sheesh, are you blind?"

I put my thick glasses back on, willing myself not to let the remark get to me.

He fell silent.

I waited to see if he'd send me on my way.

Rain pelted the windows.

I hoped he'd invite me to see the next slide.

"We had extra frogs left over from biology," Will said, as he looked through the eyepiece, "but they keep those. They're long dead anyway. And live creatures are more interesting."

Something about the way he said that bothered me. Still, I wanted to push on, having not forgotten that I had his attention only because there was no one else around. I wanted to impress my big brother.

"What else can you change?" I asked.

"Nothing, yet," he said, standing back and gesturing to the microscope.

This time, adjusting the focus was easier. I wished I'd paid attention to where the knob had been set, so I could change it back before his next turn. This planaria had two developed heads and a third, oddly shaped bit, like the stump on old man McCary's hand. Jimmy told me McCary had lost the finger in the war.

"Sometimes it doesn't work right," Will said, then suddenly brightened. "Mrs. Brewer said she'd give me some eggs in the spring." He walked around the bookcases to stand in front of the window. On a clear day, you could see the edge of Mrs. Brewer's farm up the hill. The rain came down heavily, and the warmth inside had fogged the glass.

"What can you do with eggs?"

"You can make chicks," he answered, still looking out the window.

"Can I have one?"

"If I have some I don't use."

"What about the ones you're done with?"

"You wouldn't want those," he said ominously, and turned to me. "I'm hungry! Ma left stuff for burgers. I'm having two. Want one? No buns, but we have bread." Walking past me, he turned off the lights, and waited for me. Once we'd gone out, he locked the door behind us.

I sat at the kitchen table while he slapped and shaped the ground meat into patties. He plopped them into the skillet. They sizzled immediately. My brother knew how to cook three things; scrambled eggs, bacon, and burgers. Soon enough, the greasy smell of searing beef fat reached me.

I pictured a little blue chick, like the ones they sell outside Woolworths at Easter, except this one had two heads—anything but cute. My mind followed as it ran among regular chicks and adults in an imaginary farmyard. The creature stumbled a lot, sometimes seeming frozen in place, perhaps when its two heads wanted to go in opposite directions. Hens, pecking at the pebbles in the dirt, used their sharp beaks to ward off the two-headed chick whenever it got near.

With those thoughts, I didn't much want a burger. Though, again, Will had *noticed* me, was *speaking* to me, and even the horror of the imaginary blue chick wouldn't shake me from that. Like the dog that caught the car, I had to roll with it.

"What's the freakiest thing you ever saw?" I asked.

The clock on the wall beside the refrigerator said half past 6pm. Night had fallen like a curtain. Will turned off the gas and slapped six slices of bread down, four on his plate, two on mine. He carefully lifted burgers onto our plates and carried them to the table. I'd gotten out a couple of forks and a bottle of ketchup.

"Freakiest thing, huh," he said, sitting down across from me and opening a big bag of potato chips. He took a bite from his burger, said with his mouth full, "An almost dead baby," then resumed chewing. "You weren't even born yet. Ruth was here, and Grandma, everyone in a tizzy. Mama crying and screaming like you wouldn't believe. She was having a baby—the one before you. Bet'cha didn't know about that, huh?"

"Yeah, Daddy told me," I said flatly and took a big bite of my burger the way I'd seen Will do.

He looked at me and chuckled. "Okay, anyway, the baby was early, and something was bad wrong with it. They shooed me out, told me to go outside until they said different. They thought I was still outside, but I wasn't. I'm not always where people think I am. I see a lot of things maybe I'm not supposed to…" He trailed off and his jaw twitched, like it did sometimes when Daddy went over his list of *how things are around here.*

So Will snuck around too. I don't know why I liked hearing that, especially since it meant he might know things about me. I suppose maybe I liked finding out he wasn't so different from me.

Pushing my plate away, the burger half-eaten, I planted my elbows on the table and waited while Will took a long, gulping drink of water. He looked past me.

"I saw the thing before they wrapped it up, all purple, and bloody-looking, with little black fingers. It was barely breathing, its little chest, with the ribs standing out, going up and down. It looked just like one of those eggs with the almost chick inside. I've seen a couple of those at Mrs. Brewers."

"Like, Treat with Feet?" I asked, feeling stupid the moment the words left me. I was trying to sound tough, like I knew all about it, which wasn't at all true. I knew the bit Chet had told me about the dish: A baby duck, cooked in the eggshell, and eaten with vinegar. He knew that much because his brother learned of it when he'd gone to fight in Vietnam. I'd blurted out the first gross thing I'd thought of.

"No, not like *Treat with Feet*, dumbass. Stop hanging around with that loser, Chet. Those Boyds are all weirdos. His dad wears love beads, and cries all the time 'cause he's stoned on grass."

"You're a liar," I told Will, but without any salt because the brother insults were a comfort following the hollow-eyed look he'd had minutes earlier.

"The baby," he said, "was such a little thing, undeveloped, and I didn't think it would live." He picked up his second burger, then put it down again.

"No, I'm wrong," he said. "That's the second weirdest thing. The first was seeing Mama sitting on the floor after they took the baby from her. She was holding that rabbit like it would save her from drowning."

"What rabbit?" I asked.

"You know, your stuffed rabbit. You used to carry it everywhere."

"…Bunny? Before I was born…?"

"Will nodded, picked up the hamburger, took a bite, and again spoke with his mouth full. "Grandma wrapped the baby up quick and headed outside. She stopped at the doorway to look at Ruth. They stared at each other. And this is *really* weird—I thought they hissed, or spit or something." He swallowed, and lifted his hands in a shrug. Grease from the hamburger in his left hand ran down his forearm. "Like I said, I was still a little brat and it could be mixed up in my head."

Not that weird, I thought. I'd spent a lot more time with Annie Maude than he had. Sounded like anger over *something.* Could that have been what led to their falling out?

"Even after all that Wild Kingdom stuff, Ruth wrapped Grandma and the baby in her own shawl and they left the house. Before the door closed completely, I saw something outside."

My brother had a look I'd rarely seen on him before—like the memory unsettled him.

The rain had stopped. I hadn't noticed until that moment. I hugged myself against the cold in the kitchen.

"What did you see?" I whispered in the quiet.

An uncomfortable pause as Will looked past me, maybe into memory. He sat up straighter and focused on me.

"A long, black car, kind of fancy, sat there, waiting. A man, all dressed in black, held the door open."

In Ruth's garden, wanting to know about the falling out, I'd asked, "What did Grandma do?" Ruth said, "Let's just say that no good comes from bargaining with that fellow."

Did someone make a bargain? I shivered at the thought.

"…Did the man wear a black fedora?" I asked.

"Idiot," Will said, his bumptious impatience more than I could bear. "What does that have to do with anything?"

"*Did he?*" I shrieked.

That got his attention. He looked at me squarely, and I saw some small respect for me in his eyes. Will put his burger down, composed himself, and lean forward on the table.

"I don't remember, *shit-ass.*"

I let out my breath, unaware until then I'd been holding it.

"Anyway, the baby died, just like I'd thought it would."

I could feel myself turning away from questions about the man in the black fedora, as if my mind could not hold onto what I knew of him. Were my recollections too soft on the edges? I remembered his clothing, but could not specifically recall his handsome features.

With the distraction of having found the final pieces of two puzzles, I again turned away from thoughts of the man. For one, all I'd learned about Bunny; the stuff Penny had said, what Grandma had tried not to say, and what Will had revealed told me that the stuffed rabbit had been meant for Penny. And for the other, I hadn't just thought to call the ghost girl that on a whim, like I'd always believed. Penny was her true name, and though a ghost, she was my sister.

The Night Crows and The Train
1969

I woke up feeling good because I'd be spending the day with Chet at the river. Passing through the dining room on my way to breakfast, I saw a dress pattern and cloth Mama had left on the dining room table. Looking over the pattern and her choice of cloth—a blue and green paisley—I knew she planned a new dress for me and I saw embarrassment looming in my future. I still felt the sting of the last time Mama had me wear one of her hand-made dresses. The recollection ran through me like electricity all morning and my good mood darkened. No way would I let that happen again. That ugly dress would never be, because I decided to toss the whole project in the river.

After breakfast, waiting for eleven o'clock to meet up with Chet, I tried to watch H. R. Pufnstuf. The show was for little kids, though, and I couldn't find anything on the other two stations that I wanted to watch. Returning to my room and opening a book, I found I'd grown too restless to read. I listened impatiently for my parents to leave. With them gone, I'd be able to smuggle the cloth and pattern out in a bag.

I lay on my bed, willing my parents to leave. Mama had an appointment and they'd be gone all afternoon—*if they'd just go a'ready!* They wasted a lot of time arguing over whether the small hole in the bottom of Daddy's right shoe would be noticeable.

Finally, I heard the back door open and close. The car started up in the driveway and pulled away—my chance.

I reached out for my lucky penny, which lay on the fireplace mantle in my room, but hesitated and then decided to leave it, because I didn't want to lose the coin if I took a fall in the river.

Ruth would be downstairs—I'd heard her arrive. She'd be ironing, taking little nips from the flask she kept in her apron pocket, laughing at some soap opera, and wouldn't pay me any mind. A weekend day, Will might sleep till dark. Ruth had never bothered much about the doings of us kids if we showed up for meals on time and more or less intact. Her children had all grown up. They didn't die from their adventures, so I guess she figured we wouldn't from ours.

In the dining room, I gathered up the dress pattern, the cloth, and even the pins and thread. In the kitchen, I stuffed all that into a brown grocery bag, and made a peanut butter and jelly sandwich to take with me.

Ruth had put the ironing board in the living room so she could work while watching her shows. She sprinkled water from a soda bottle with holes punched through its metal cap, spattering a shirt front. She pressed the iron down. Steam rose around her.

"I'll be at Chet's," I told her.

Smiling and pointing the bottle at me, she said, "Be back before the four-thirty. Your mama wants to serve dinner early so she and your daddy can go out tonight."

The kids in my neighborhood didn't need watches. We had the train horns and mill whistles.

I went out and clomped down the steps with the bag under my arm.

~ ~ ~

Following lunch—he'd brought a mustard and cheese sandwich (yuck!)—Chet and I crawled on our knees through the deep blackberry hedge that lined a certain secluded section of the riverbank. Though grumpy, Chet endured the the thorny bramble for me. I didn't want anyone to see what I was about to do, if only to avoid being seen littering the river. In summer, the blackberry vines were weighted down with clusters of fat berries and buzzing with yellow jackets. Now, in a hot mid-fall, the birds had plucked away all the fruit, and just the growth remained, a maze of dry thorns out for blood. We got through with a few nasty scratches, and plenty of dirty words. A couple of red spots bloomed on Chet's sleeve, and I had a stinging scratch on my cheek. The heat and my sweat getting into the wound made it worse.

I pulled my shoes off and rolled my pants up to my knees, before stepping into the chilly river. Even on the hottest days, the water stayed cold.

We put a couple of rocks in the bag that held Mama's sewing project to add weight. I meant to throw the sack into the center of the fast-moving current, about thirty feet out. As I swung, one of the rocks tore through the bottom. Without the weight, my throw fell embarrassingly short. The bag disintegrated in the water, the other rock and the pins must have sunk, and the green and blue paisley cloth and dress pattern meandered downstream.

Chet and I watched them go, saw the hateful cloth get caught on a branch. Like a mocking gesture, the fabric waved in the current like a flag.

I wouldn't have it. Though highly unlikely, I feared someone else rescuing the cloth and Mama somehow finding out about what I'd done. Silly, considering she'd suspect me first when her project turned up missing. Even so, I wanted that fabric gone, sunk, maybe even washed out to sea.

Chet and I argued about how to retrieve the cloth, since it looked like somebody would have to get wet. Finally, his idea won out. He took off his belt and cinched one end around my left ankle.

"Chet, you better not let go." I took two steps out into water that rose to my knees. Pushing my luck, I leaned way out toward the fast-moving current, where the water got much deeper. If Daddy found out about the risk I took, I'd be picking the switch he would swat me with. But I could almost reach my prize, and there's nothing more dangerous for me than getting within a hair's breadth of something I truly want. Right arm out, left hand back and over my head, I stood on my right foot like a tightrope walker. Chet kept hold of the belt around my left ankle. I dug my toes into the mud under the moving water, stretching as far as I could, while betting my safety on the grip and loyalty of an eleven-year-old. Chet adjusted his hands on the belt, leaning back.

"Don't you dare let go, asshole!" I shouted over the river noise.

"You hankerin' for a little swim?" he asked. "I told you to let *me* throw it."

I wobbled then, did a little "aeroplaning" to regain my balance. Laughing, Chet threw his head back, and let the belt slip. Figuring he'd let go, I decided to snag the bag and take it with me.

"Got it!" I said, expecting the river's cold embrace next.

Instead, the grip on my ankle tightened. Just as my right elbow dipped into the water, I stopped falling.

The motion of a crow caught my eye.

No—a mistake—not a bird. Turned out to be a man upriver, dressed in a fine black suit.

Him, again! Him and that hateful fedora.

I felt off-kilter, like in a tilt house, when you think the floor is crooked and it's really the walls. I got a bad twinge in my stomach.

I didn't think the man had seen me and had to hide before he did.

"Pull me back," I said, "*now!*"

"My mind on the man, I didn't much hear Chet's smart-ass come back, something about me needing a bath.

The black figure climbed wooden steps that led up the embankment beside a gravel boat ramp upstream. The river made a slight curve there. A few inches difference would keep me out of sight.

"Pull me *back*, asshole!"

All Chet had for me was laughter.

The man took two steps up the stairs. I lost sight of him behind trees and shrubs growing along the bank.

Relieved, I let out my breath.

Chet pulled me back.

Hopping out of the water onto the bank, I loosened the belt and threw it at him.

His grin begged to be slapped. He couldn't know why I'd become so upset, and for some reason, I didn't want to tell him.

I held up the sopping cloth, now looking more sad than hateful.

Glancing around, I worried the man might be hidden somewhere nearby.

"Okay," Chet said, rubbing his palms together. "Let's do it right this time. I'll get some more rocks and we'll tie it up with those inside. We'll go up on the trestle and sling it!" He started pushing his belt back through his pant loops with a look of satisfaction—his idea of using the belt had worked, after all.

Keeping my eyes on my bare feet while dragging them through a patch of grass, I worked at rubbing the mud off before putting my shoes back on. I took my time, hoping the man in the black fedora had kept walking away.

"My stomach kinda hurts," I said. "I think I'm gonna go home."

"What? After all that? It'll take two shakes!"

How could I tell him about the man in the black fedora?

"I'll sling it way out to the middle." Still pumped up, he pantomimed, looking like a cowboy with a lasso, or David itching to slay Goliath.

Boys!

The Sun peeking through clouds over his shoulder, I squinted up at Chet. Tying my shoes, I said, "No, let's do it later. I need to get home before the four-thirty."

I had to get away from the man in the black fedora.

Chet dropped his arms and shoulders in exaggerated disappointment.

"Go home then, *weirdo*." He walked a few steps ahead, and turned back with a longish look. He frowned, tilting his head to one side. "You all right? Wanna come to my house?" Chet wiped his hand on his pants and offered to pull me up.

"Nah. Ruth will be mad. Meet me at the trestle after supper. Then we'll throw it in right."

I picked up the paisley cloth and squeezed more water out of it. We walked silently up the hill, parting ways in the alley. Glancing behind me as I went, I continued up through the garden, past the garage, and to the house.

The four-thirty train horn blew, followed by the familiar rumble. I climbed the steps to the deep, screened-in back porch that held nothing but shadows in the overcast. Light spilled out of the kitchen window. I heard tinny music from a radio and smelled hambone and tomato soup. Surprised, I stopped, my hand on the doorknob. Hambone soup meant Ruth cooked. Ruth cooking meant my parents wouldn't be back for dinner.

With that, I just knew that Mama had gone to the Kleckly again. And again, I had a sense of humiliation, something that, at the time, I found unaccountable.

Heavy sigh. This wasn't Mama's first visit to the Kleckly Building, part of the state hospital complex. Not a good place. What little I knew came from eavesdropping. And the low voices had meant shame came with having to go there.

Ruth stood in the kitchen, stirring the soup with a ladle. She turned a knob and the blue flame under the big pot shrank to nothing.

"What's this?" she asked, pointing at the paisley cloth. I'd forgot—still clung to the fabric absentmindedly. Water dripped from it onto the worn linoleum.

"So *that's* where that cloth went," Ruth said. "Give it to me." She took the cloth and wrung it out over the sink, shaking her head. "We'll reckon with that later. Go wash and get to the table."

When I returned, a bowl of the hot soup, thick with rice, chunks of ham, and tomato waited for me at the kitchen table, along with a glass of milk and two slices of white bread.

I sat, knowing I was in trouble. Ruth might not scold me, but when Mama heard about what I'd done, there'd be hell to pay.

"Your Daddy will be home tomorrow. Your Mama will be home another day or two later." Ruth stood with her back to me. I quietly lifted the salt shaker. Before I could get any salt in my soup, she turned around and grabbed the shaker right out of my hand and put it on the counter. She took the pepper too. She knew me well. I would over-salt the soup and be up and down all night, going for water, watching and listening for things she said should remain unnoticed. She turned back to folding dishcloths with precise, mechanical movements.

"Mama's at the Kleckly," I said to her back.

She stopped and turned more slowly this time, crossing her arms. She wore a bandana tied around her wiry white hair. Her dress was olive green, with tiny pink flowers, a little faded, yet neatly starched. Her dark skin almost hid the circles under eyes that were now fixed on me. I looked at the familiar pink scars on her forearms. They fascinated me, as did her pale, deeply lined palms.

"What do you know about that? "she asked.

I shifted my feet on the floor, remembering a time they wouldn't quite reach. I wondered if, when Ruth noticed the mud on my shoes, she'd make me spill the story about the paisley cloth.

"It's a place for crazy people, *like a jail*," I said. I squished a bit of white bread into a dense little cube. To get the edges sharp, I had to focus. She didn't tell me to stop.

Instead, she pulled out a chair and sat down carefully.

The kitchen had grown steamy from the cooking. Ruth reached into a drawer behind her and pulled out a church fan, a rounded square of white cardboard, stapled onto a thin wooden handle. One side had the words, "Compliments of Posey's Funeral Home, since 1947," printed on it in a churchy script.

The other side had a picture of a dark-skinned Jesus holding a lamb. I'd always been fascinated by that too. She fanned herself with long, full strokes. I sighed unselfconsciously and popped the chewy cube of bread into my mouth.

"You don't tell nobody what I tell you now," Ruth said. "And I mean *No* body." She looked at me, her dark eyes serious.

By "nobody," I had a feeling she meant Grandma.

The radio droned on. The light outside had darkened a little more. I tore off another bit of bread to squish. The fan had stopped moving.

I looked up at her and solemnly nodded my consent. The fanning resumed.

"It all started with the Crows," she said, looking out the window into the growing twilight. "That was the first time they took your mama to the *Kleckly* place.

"Them birds, they are clever, them crows. They're always around, but that one week, they were all over them pecan trees out back. Looked like black leaves. Seems like every crow in town was right here in them trees. But that *weren't* so. Every crow in town was in everybody else's trees too, night and day. The *noise!* Then they got up on the roof of this very house, squawking and pecking, dropping rocks and nut shells down the chimney. The racket come down hard on your mama. She about pulled her hair out. She went under her bed and curled up in a knot. Wouldn't answer me nor move an inch. Whined like an animal when I pulled at her. I couldn't see nothing but them bony elbows of hers. So, I come in here to the phone and called the mill. Told the foreman to send your daddy home." Ruth stared off toward the window, slowly shaking her head. "You were a baby, still in the crib." At that, she smiled, as if remembering me small. Her expression darkened, and she went on. "When I went back upstairs, your brother and sister were standing at the door, looking in. They'd been in a play at school. Both were wearing rabbit suits made of old sheets. Had coat hangers in the ears so they stood up straight. I couldn't see their faces, just them droopy cotton tails. What I saw was two little bunnies, looking in that room, trying to put that knot under the bed together with their mama. They held hands, like all they had in the world was each other. And right then, that was true. First, their own daddy dying like he did, and now they mama gone in the head."

Ruth put her fan down, laid her palms flat on the table.

"Look at me, girl. Your mama believed something was wrong about them crows. Something *bad* wrong. She took that it had something to do with her. But everybody else believed them crows were just *crows*, and something was bad wrong with your mama."

I sat in silence, trying to take all that in. I placed the new bread cube gently on the table. Ruth lifted one hand and covered my smaller one. I looked down at the cube. Its edges ran sharp and straight. I remembered hearing the car pull away across the gravel that morning, and me, upstairs, not saying goodbye to Mama.

Ruth took both my hands. "*I* believe everybody *else* was wrong. And so does your grandma."

I looked hard at her.

"Now," she said, and paused, standing and smoothing her apron, "finish your supper and tell me about this sopping-wet cloth in the sink. And I expect you'll tell me where the rest of your mother's sewing needs went."

While I'd have to tell her they were lost and I knew she would tell Mama I'd ruined the sewing project, I didn't hold it against Ruth. That was part of the job she'd been hired to do. I had a hard time imagining anything threatening our friendship. We talked about a number of other things until about five-thirty, when I thought to look at the clock.

Chet—I'd forgotten him!

Jumping up, I shoved my chair back under the table, said, "Gotta go!" I ran out, letting the screen door slam behind me, and hurried toward the alley.

Even though Ruth hadn't tried to stop me, her disturbing tale chased me down the alley and through the trees, into the fading light.

~ ~ ~

Dusk fell as I stood on the train trestle. Chet was late, an unusual thing for him. I walked farther onto the trestle than I should have, to watch for his approach. That far out, I could see the tip of Chet's roof through the trees. From there, he would be a tiny figure if I saw him at all through the leafy obstructions, so I kept my eyes at the edge of the trees where I knew his path emerged from the woods.

I'd grown eager to tell him my mother had been taken to the asylum. That particular something felt too big to hold onto. I wanted to blurt it out. To be honest, I looked forward to the measure of awe and bit of sympathy the news would get me. In my limited world of dungarees and bubblegum, both were valuable commodities.

I tried to sort through my feelings about Mama being at the Kleckly, but instead, my head filled with worries for her in that terrible place. I imagined her being mistreated, being frightened of the others there, being kept there against her will.

A prickling in the soles of my feet warned of the six o'clock train coming as I saw the man, all in black and wearing a hat, walking toward me. I glanced around quickly. Not another soul in sight.

Though the man's face remained hidden in the shadow of his hat's brim, the light caught the gleam on his shoes. A memory I'd hid away tumbled out: The man in the black fedora kept his wingtips shined like that.

"Go away!" I yelled.

Then Ruth's words came back to me: "You talk to him and he'll never leave you be."

I clapped a hand over my mouth.

Mama had spoken to him too....

The gravity of my situation brought me back to where I stood. I'd walked too far out on the trestle with a train coming, and had little space to shield myself. Since continuing the same way would take even longer, my exit lay beyond the man I considered a danger. Some effort had been required to persuade my younger self that he wasn't a monster, only a man, at worst, a criminal. Yet, in my gut, I'd never been fooled. Monsters were real, and the man in the black fedora was one of them. So was the six o'clock train.

Jumping in the river wasn't an option—falling from that height, I'd be killed when I struck the bedrock at the bottom. I looked to the meager space on the other side of the tracks. A little wider than where I stood, but not by much. I needed to get off the tracks right away.

Wanting to run, I instead turned and walked toward him, trying to seem at ease. Nervously, my hands opened and closed on their own. Even as I willed myself not to look at the man, I fixed upon those blue eyes. His sudden smile, like a knife, pared away all my denial, and I knew again the primitive dread that came with his presence on the first day we'd met.

I stopped and wrapped my arms around one of the bridge's iron girders. I held on and resorted to the last defense of a child, no better than hiding under bedsheets—I refused to acknowledge the man's presence. The old, heavily-textured metal I hugged stood solid, while I felt fragile as one of Mrs. Boyd's glass animals. If I shivered, I would surely break. I kept my eyes fixed on the metal beam, praying for my friend to show. I held my breath—like that would help!

And maybe it did—a glance revealed Chet's small figure coming out of the trees and hurrying down the path. I let go of the girder, and waved my arms over my head to get his attention.

"Tick tock, Butterscotch," said the monster in my ear. The train horn blew, loud and close. Chet heard the horn too and broke into a run.

The train burst out of the trees and clattered onto the trestle, bearing down. Years of my father's instructions leapt up from somewhere in the back of my brain. In six steps, I got to the narrow ledge on the other side of the tracks. I pressed myself down flat against the supports and as far from the track as possible, covering my head with my arms. The whole world shook. I smelled the grease and hot metal, felt the pull of the moving train like the sucking wind of a tornado that wanted to yank me up, tear me out of my clothes, and toss me away. Pebbles flew at me, a few pelting my back. One struck me sharply on the back of my head. The rest rained down into the water below. The passing rail cars seemed to go on forever. I became numb.

And then, the oddest thing: part of me wanted to let go, believing I'd fly along behind the train like a girl-shaped helium balloon tethered to the caboose.

Finally, the iron flying by, the roar, the whipping dust, and pelting rocks ended. The next sounding of the horn came lower in pitch and fading. The man in the black fedora was nowhere in sight. Chet crouched on the tracks not far away, bent over with his hands on his knees, breathing hard.

He approached and plopped down beside me. "You scared the…" He took deep breaths. "…Hell out of me!" Chet rubbed his hands over his face.

I sat up. "Where *were* you?" I shouted at him, and burst into tears, leaving him, I'm sure, with no idea what to do next. He pulled a handkerchief out of his pocket, seemed to reconsider, and poked it back in.

He would grow up to teach religious studies at the university in Charleston. He would become a fine husband, a loving father, respected in his community. That man already sat beside me in character.

"What were you doing way out here?" he asked.

"Waitin' for you!" I said through tears. "The man in... black. Where did he go?"

"What man?" he yelled. "I didn't see any man! Just you, way out here like a-an idiot!"

I looked around for the man. No, the *monster*. I heard the words again in my mind, "Tick Tock, butterscotch."

Leaning over the edge, I heaved my hambone soup into the river. Even after spitting out all I could, my mouth felt gritty. I wiped my face on my sleeve. We sat quietly for a minute.

"You must be gettin' sick," he said. "Come on, let's go. Your mama will be worried."

He didn't know yet that she'd gone to the Kleckly.

We stood and he looked at me.

"You're a mess," he said, "covered in dirt. Your mother's gonna call mine and I'll be in the shit too!"

"She's not home." I said. "Ruth is there. I'm okay." I let the subject go at that. I didn't want to talk anymore.

We started for home. I got to the end of the trestle before he did. Looking back, I wondered if I'd ever want to be on the tracks again. Though I'd stopped crying, I hitched and sniffed.

Chet put an arm over my shoulders. "So, how was the six o'clock up close?" he asked.

"You're an asshole," I said, "and I forgot the paisley cloth."

He looked confused for a second, then chuckled. "I forgot all about that." Didn't matter anymore.

He stopped suddenly as we stepped off the trestle.

"Hey, I meant to tell you…" he said, turning to me. He wiped his face again. "…something weird is going on." Chet had grown fidgety, excited.

"What sort of weird?" I asked.

"In town. The birds are acting funny. The crows. They're in the trees, on the wires, crapping on everything. On people's cars. At night!" he gestured up at the darkening sky. The clouds still hung low. "Tommy and them clods shot some of 'em dead with BB guns. The rest didn't even fly away! Just got quiet for a minute and then started right up again. Ma said this happened before when I was a baby. They give her the heebie-jeebies. When I wanted to go out, she had a conniption fit. That's why I was late. I had to sneak out my window." He shoved his hands deep into his pockets.

I stared at him in dumb silence. Chet was one week older than me. His mother had told him about the same crow storm that sent Mama to the Kleckly place, shortly after my birth. A couple of the large birds landed on the dock below, watching us. Another perched like a sentinel on a streetlamp nearby. Seeing its black eye staring at me, I shivered, and the unexpected thought came that I'd better give Bunny to Penny, or else.

"Hey, you okay?" Chet said, the second time he'd asked that in one day. I nodded.

We looked toward the trees that stood between us and our houses.

"They're everywhere," he said. "Just listen to 'em."

And I did. I listened and found myself wanting to curl up and hide.

"Mama." I whispered.

~ ~ ~

I'd made my decision or the choice had been made for me. I left Bunny on the chair beside the grandfather clock in the hall that night. Shortly after, the stuffed animal had disappeared. I didn't want to look for it. Instead, I quietly asked Ruth and Will if they knew what had become of Bunny. They did not.

Later, while passing through the hall, I saw something on the chair. Bunny's button eye lay upon the seat, the one that had come off several times before. This time, there was a bit of Bunny's fabric still attached by the fishing line last used to hold the button in place, as if the eye had been bitten off. I thought of Penny's little teeth.

The Tree
1970

I tore the bag open, and folds of blue vinyl spilled out with a smooth hiss. Along with the plastic smell, memories of Edisto Beach flooded out: of sun, crashing waves, and wet sand, blindingly bright. Seagulls cried overhead and I bobbed on the cold water, my head turned to watch the next wave grow from the flat, endless line of sea and sky behind me. My legs squeaked against the float as I readied to catch the next breaker, hoping to be swept along in the salty foam, all the way back to the sand. My eagerness—a psalm of unblemished joy. My heart sang to the surf's roar…the beach…the ocean…the wonder.

Only memories…

I gazed sullenly down the row of tents. The campsite provided all the necessities, no amenities. The spaces were more or less lined up in rows between the pines, marked off by gravel pathways. Each had a picnic table, a grill, and an old, industrial drum to serve as trash can. The drums had the space numbers spray-painted on them. Lights hung from poles distributed somewhat randomly. About a third of the spaces had occupants.

On the way in, we'd passed a playground, empty but for a boy with wild red hair hanging upside down from the monkey bars. His green and white striped tee shirt had slid down and he scratched his ribs on both sides like an ape.

No rain had fallen that week. The ground had grown dusty, with scattered carpets of dry pine needles. Chiggers would be hiding in there. My ankles would be dotted with pink calamine soon enough. Or, if Mama had forgotten to pack that, then nail polish. She always had nail polish.

We'd pitched our three tents in spaces five, six, and seven. The closest other campers were three spaces away.

This *wasn't* the ocean…

I wouldn't be catching waves with my new, sky-blue float. I'd be lying on it in the cramped, humid tent, jammed up next to my snoring brother on his red one, and listening to choruses of crickets. Four long nights like that, and longer, sweaty days of mosquito bites, gnats buzzing around my ears, and raw, dull-eyed boredom.

The one thing that could make the fish camp bearable would be exploring the surrounding woods. The trees had been there long before the dirty campground, the noisy campers, and the bad smells they brought with them. The wind, the rustling leaves, the occasional moan of bending branches and trunks spoke to me. I belonged, and that belonging felt good.

But that kind of exploration was now forbidden, since I'd disappeared into the woods for *five minutes* the last time we'd come Santee Cooper.

"Look how you've upset your mother," Daddy had said when they finally found me. "You've frightened us all."

Mama dabbed at her red-rimmed eyes and wet nose with her stupid scarf. More than fright, I saw anger. I got no relieved hugging, no grateful smiles.

"You've ruined the whole trip for everyone," she said. "Your aunts and uncles are beside themselves, worried sick."

If they worried so much about me, where were they? And Mama, she just needed to put on a show that she loved me.

I looked to my brother, hoping for some understanding. He looked embarrassed, shoved his hands in his pockets, and studied his shoes.

Despite having some sympathy for Mama, after what I'd learned of her emotional problems, I considered her a poor mother at best. I did love her, even though she made that hard much of the time.

Returning to our campsite, we discovered my aunts and uncles playing cards, having what Daddy would have called "a big time." They cheered and raised their cups when we appeared.

My punishment had been grounding in the tent for the rest of the day. That trip had been maybe a year earlier.

Since setting up camp in the morning, I found myself stuck on the bank with Mama and my aunts, Aldean and Jewel. They would fish from the bank while Daddy and my uncles—his brothers—fished from two small jon boats down where the creek fed into the lake. My brother had gone with them.

Of course, he had…

Daddy had said, "finish blowing up your floats before coming down to the water. You won't want to do it tonight." My brother had finished first and gone without me. In a hurry, I'd tried too hard, making myself dizzy. By the time I'd steadied myself, grabbed my lifejacket, and hurried to the water's edge, the boats were already out of sight. I wouldn't even get a glimpse of the lake that day.

I'd begged for the beach for two weeks. Not even giving up my allowance and doing extra chores would change their minds. "Next time," Daddy had said, patting my shoulder, and chuckling in a way that told me he didn't take me seriously. That was it, then. Dismissed.

I hated those family fishing trips....

The single-day outings to fish with just Daddy and me had always been the best. We'd done that since I was six. I liked fishing below the train trestle best. He'd teach me things about the trains, all from his own experience; like how to get on and off safely, their schedules, and about the hobos that jumped the trains and rode all over the country during the depression. Whenever a locomotive went across the trestle while we fished beneath, Daddy bent over me to give some protection from the gravel that fell from above.

On the day we made our lucky pennies, we'd returned to the bank and climbed up to the tracks to look for railroad spikes. He found a bent one and I found a straight one. He gave me his to keep.

In those outings, Daddy became my pal and my protector.

So why would he leave me behind now, without a word?

Why couldn't I go out on the boats too? I could've sat on the ice chest in the middle.

Daddy had probably known I couldn't get the float blown up in time...

The boat had room enough for me...!

Though I fished better than Will, he had the advantage of being older and a *boy*.

My eyes shot imaginary daggers to follow them.

The day had already turned hot. My fishing pole rested on a log near Mama's chair. I didn't want to fish. I couldn't imagine why the grownups wanted to come to Santee Cooper, a place of miserable heat and humidity that time of year. The fine silt, picked up and blown by even the slightest breeze, stuck to our sweaty skin, collecting inside our elbows and around our necks. The insects never let up, especially the gnats in my face.

But the camp spaces came dirt cheap in August, and they considered the fishing "mighty good." Mighty good out on the water in a boat, maybe. On the bank, fishing was mighty crappy.

I let out a long sigh, picked my pole up off the log. From the old coffee can full of loamy soil that sat on the ground, I chose a doomed nightcrawler to impale on my hook. I picked a lively one over a fatter, slow one and pressed the barbed point into the worm's tough band until the sharp metal popped through the other side. Of course, even the slow ones wriggled when the hook went in. I swung the line out until the hooked worm and sinker plopped into the water. I'd slid the cork way up the line so the bait went deep. Catfish were bottom feeders, not too choosy about the bait, and—more importantly— Daddy hated skinning catfish. If I had to fish on that shitty bank, then he'd have to bring out his heavy pliers and gloves to clean my catch.

Even though I wasn't interested in the women's conversation, their loud cackling kept snagging me. Something about their tone didn't feel right. These women wore pastel dresses and pristine white gloves at Easter and pretended to be *oh so proper*. Yet now they seemed *naked*. I felt like I didn't know them.

Aunt Aldean wore a loose shirt and no brassiere. The skin between her breasts was browned and wrinkled. She laughed behind her hand like she'd said something naughty. And maybe she had—what would I know about such things?

Aunt Jewel leaned back in one of those folding aluminum lounge chairs. She wore a broad sun hat. Following the line of her tanned legs up to her shorts, I saw dark, curling hair peeking out at the fabric's edge. She opened a bottle of Coca-Cola, unfolded the paper ends of a headache powder, and carefully tapped the white stuff into the drink. As she settled the bottle between her thighs, right next to that hair, the liquid inside foamed up and rose to leak out the top and flow over her hand.

"Oh, look at me," she cried, with an obnoxious guffaw. "Look what I can do." She thrust her hips a bit, and I got the impression maybe she pretended to be a boy. Mama and Aunt Aldean were also laughing way too loudly.

Had they forgot I stood nearby? Weren't they supposed to be a good example?

Hadn't Aunt Jewel been the one to shame me for running around without my underpants? I couldn't have been more than six at the time. The sting of her hand on my bare butt had been a warning I remembered. Later, when my cousins all went skinny-dipping at Clark's Hill, I didn't join in, and sat alone, watching their shameless fun from the pier. That sting also prompted me to always tuck my skirts around my legs tightly, and to make sure I locked bathroom doors.

And now, looking at Mama, I saw she liked all that talk, found it funny. What next, then? The thought came that she'd be stepping out with the man in the black fedora and Daddy's heart would be broken. Would that be the first time she'd done that?

But that couldn't be. That fellow wasn't an ordinary man—a lover—was he?

Surprised at the thought, I said aloud, "No, he's a monster!"

They all looked at me, and I shrugged for them.

Aunt Jewel crumpled the powder paper and tossed it behind her. "Breakfast of champions!" she said, lifting her bottle to tap against Mama's. Aunt Jewel turned up her Coca-Cola and drank lustily. Her throat moved with each swallow. Mama and Aunt Aldean watched with uncouth grins.

"So, you overdid it last night, did you?" Mama asked with a chuckle.

Even at the age of twelve, I asked myself why I should let those adults tell *me* how to act?

~ ~ ~

In late afternoon, the boats returned, and we all trudged back to the camp.

Passing by, Daddy lifted my stringer to look at my catch—three good-sized fish. "Catfish, huh?" he said, his tone teasing. He noticed how I'd strung them. Instead of passing the stringer through the gills, which would kill them quickly, I'd cut slits in the flesh under their throats and passed the metal line through the openings, then out through their mouths. That kept them alive, fresher, longer, as they dangled in the cold water. That sort of thing didn't bother me like it did other girls. Besides, fish were like worms, I reminded myself, they didn't really feel anything. With Daddy's slight smile, I knew I'd pleased him. Maybe I'd *imagined* he didn't want me to go out in the boats. I felt a little tingle of pride and saw myself out on the lake next time.

The men would clean some of the catch for dinner and put the rest in big, insulated chests. Ice could be replenished at the small market and bait shop a short walk down the dirt road that ran through the camp. You could get a fishing license there, basic provisions, and camping supplies, but no booze.

On the way to camp, we'd stopped where the dirt road joined the main one. A gas station occupied one corner, and a white building, painted with big red dots, sat across the road on an otherwise empty lot. The men had gone into that building, while the rest of us waited in the cars. They came back carrying two cardboard boxes they stowed in one of the boats before driving on.

Beside the camp's market, a concrete structure provided toilet and cold shower facilities. Signs reminded campers to wear bathing suits in the showers. Although the toilets were clean, you had to bring your own paper. I headed there with the women to shower and change before dinner.

~ ~ ~

For all my ill-tempered, self-imposed misery through the day, I had to admit that the fried fish, hushpuppies, and slaw tasted great, the plates heaped full.

After all that sun and food, I turned sleepy. Before turning in for the night, I peed in the grass behind our tent. The campground lights came on before I went back in. The streaks of cold cream, meant to ease my sunburn, appeared shiny and blue in the dim light. The stuff felt so cold when I'd slathered it on. Now the cold cream had grown cakey. My tender skin stuck to the plastic. I couldn't get comfortable.

I rolled to my side, hoping for a breeze through the open tent flap. From where I lay, I saw my family around the picnic table. The light bulbs overhead created a glow over them, softening the colors. The warm scene could have been printed on one of those paper church fans Ruth used, except that the light left harsh shadows on their features. Though I couldn't make out their words at that distance, the talk again sounded coarse. They all appeared to be having a high time except for Daddy, who seemed thoughtful. He sat off to one side smoking a cigarette, as if he were by himself. Every now and then, Mama would put her hands over my brother's ears, maybe playfully, right before the rest of them broke out in loud laughter. Her smile grew too big. My uncles laughed too hard.

~ ~ ~

An animal cry awoke me some time later. The crickets had stopped singing. I lay unmoving in the still darkness, listening like I did so often in the night at home. Of course, *she* hadn't come with us.

Again, that animal sound—a high, keening whine. Something restless in the distance, I guessed.

But, no—I heard it again, and this time I knew the sound came from my brother, a foot or more away. I peered at him through the darkness. The sound became a whimper inside his throat that couldn't escape his closed lips, soft, and, and…

He was having *that* dream. The one about the ocean. He'd had it before. In the dream, he would be screaming.

He'd told me about it once while we waited for Mama outside the fabric store, a dull place no self-respecting kid could bear. Usually, we weren't the only kids sitting on the curb. That day we had the spot all to ourselves. With no witnesses, Will could drop his mask and be with me, as he seldom did. He sat quiet for a time, kind of fidgety, then squinted up at the sun, and said, "Ever have the same dream more than once?"

"Uh…I don't guess so."

"I dream of Edisto, on the beach at night," he said in a whisper, his eyes not quite focused on the traffic going by. "In the dream, a terrible storm is coming. The moon…it's too big. I can only see it in glimpses between the clouds. The clouds are moving fast, all together, like birds that got spooked, you know? Like they're trying to get away from something."

He paused, and pulled at his eyebrow the way he did sometimes while studying. He had my full attention. He bent down to tighten his shoelaces and continued. "The waves are deafening. I want to cover my ears, but I just stand there watching them eat up the shoreline, closing in. There are lots of people, and they're all scared. They're running around, making these huge bonfires to keep the water back. They burn everything in sight, dragging furniture and stuff from the houses, even their clothes and books."

He turned and looked me in the eye, and I knew that what he'd say next bothered him most. "All of a sudden, they drop to their knees, clasp their hands together hard and pray, begging to be saved. Moonlight falling through the fast-moving clouds is like spotlights played over the crowd. I spot Mom and Dad and try to call out, but I can't. I can't move at all. I can only stare at the sea, rising higher and higher. And I know it's all over.

"That's when I wake up, every time."

He looked at me expectantly. I had to say something *helpful.* To buy time to think, I reached in my pocket for two sticks of Fruit Stripe that grandma had given me. I offered him one and opened the other for myself.

That's a stupid *dream,* I thought. *Fire can't hold back water.* Yet I couldn't say so—he'd been seriously spooked.

Leaning in close, Will whispered, "Don't tell Daddy. He'll think I'm a pantywaist."

That was the moment I understood that Will hid his fears from Daddy like I did.

I nodded agreement—as good as a promise.

Will popped the gum into his mouth and held the wrapper loosely. I saw that the lickable tattoo that came with his stick of gum matched the one I already wore.

Grabbing and licking it quick, I slapped the tattoo on his hand and pressed hard. He didn't try to stop me.

I let go and held mine up. "Look, we're the same."

He bumped my tattoo with his, and gave me a smile.

I hadn't had to say anything in the end.

Mama came out, carrying a wrapped package. "All done!" she said. She looked pleased.

We got up and followed Mama to our car. Will sat shotgun and didn't look back at me on the way home.

That had been a moment between us, one when we forgot to pretend we hated each other.

I kept my promise, while still thinking his dream stupid. I also got to feel superior—his nightmare didn't sound scary to me at all.

Again, in the darkened tent, I heard the tortured sound come from his throat. His face, shiny with sweat in the scant light, wore a terrible grimace. I reached out and put my hand on his shoulder, shook him gently—once, twice. His eyes opened, wide and staring. I shook him again and he focused on me.

Will took a long, shuddering breath to gather his voice, glanced back to where our parents slept in their cots. "Don't tell Daddy," he whispered, "He'll think I'm soft, like that Overby guy."

He meant the fellow at the barber shop with the pretty hands that Daddy always complained about. I shook my head to reassure him.

He rolled over, away from me.

His imagined Edisto was so different from my own. I sniffed at my float to bring back the pleasant memories. The vinyl smell, nearly gone, still brought me a taste of the coast I so loved. The plastic odor must've worked differently for my brother. *Maybe he should've picked a blue float like mine.* I smiled at the thought.

The next morning, I awoke early and donned life jacket and fishing hat. I grabbed two mini boxes of cereal from our supplies, carefully opened the perforated sides, broke open the wax paper, and poured milk into each.

Bottles and paper cups littered the picnic table. Some held brownish liquid and cigarette butts. After clearing off a corner, I sat down and gobbled the cereal with a plastic spoon, then turned up each box and slurped the extra milk from the corners. By the look of the table, Aunt Jewel would be in her powders again.

I tossed the empty boxes into our site 7 barrel and headed to the creek, arriving before anyone else.

The still morning air had a chill bite. I shook off my flipflops and stepped into the shallow, cold water. The dark dot of a boat appeared downstream. Soon as it disappeared around the bend, I squatted in the water, pulling my bathing suit aside so I could pee. When I stepped back out, I shivered a little, glad for the padded life jacket.

The sun rose higher. The birds chirped in various voices. Leaves rustled in the slight breeze, and the gently moving water gurgled on. To kill time, I drew in the wet sand with a stick. I turned over rocks looking for crawfish and salamanders, but didn't find any. Bored with all that, I made a decision: Forget Dad's rules—who cared if the fish were frightened away? No one would be catching anything here anyway—the women hadn't even tried. I gathered flat rocks to skip on the water.

Winding up to skip my first stone, I heard voices behind me, growing closer. I turned to see Mama and my aunts approaching noisily, plenty loud enough to scare away any fish. They toted towels, folding beach chairs, and oversized straw bags filled with unnecessary stuff.

I let loose with a rock, a good one that skipped eight times. *Eight!*…and no Chet to see it.

"I don't know what got into Edgar," Aunt Aldean said. She held a cigarette in her fingers and bent down awkwardly to take a puff so she wouldn't drop the towels cradled in her arm. "I don't think I've ever seen him quite like that."

"I can tell you this," Mama said, "whatever's got him crabby, Alton's not over it. He was a bear this morning." She made a face. They all laughed, their voices having a nervous edge. The laughter ended all of a sudden when they spotted me.

Mama put on a big smile. "I *hoped* I'd find you here," she said, brightly.

Had she worried she'd have to drag me out of the forest again? That would ruin the whole damn trip! I simply waved.

"Hey Mama, I got eight skips, first try."

"That's nice, sweetie."

My aunts opened chairs and spread towels on them. Mama walked to me and kissed the top of my head. She gingerly touched my red shoulders. I'd smeared a generous coating of her face cream on them.

"Hmm, that might work," she said, looking from one shoulder to the other, then into my eyes. For a moment I thought she would scold me about the cream, but she didn't. She approved, and I felt *clever.*

She turned suddenly, toward the clamor of the men approaching over the crest of the bank. I stiffened, preparing to protect my rightful position on one of those boats. I'd stand my ground and speak aloud the argument I'd fashioned in my head yesterday.

Daddy appeared first, and he broke into a genuine, spontaneous grin when he saw me. As seen through the blue-tinted fake "sunglasses" fabricated into the brim of my hat, he looked like a movie star. His smile faded quickly, though, and he glanced back at my uncles. He put his gear on the ground and approached me. I held my fishing pole upright, like a flag I'd planted on the idea that I'd be on one of those damned boats. He knelt in front of me so that our faces were even. "You got up early there, Rooster," he said, tapping my life jacket gently with one finger. His shoulders slumped a little, and he took my small hands in his. "Listen, sweetie pie," he began.

Oh, no, I thought. I could feel my eyes narrow in defiance of what I saw coming.

"Today, the men have to have some grown up talk," he continued. He looked right into my eyes and said, "Tomorrow—I double-dog promise, *tomorrow*." That only made it worse.

My rehearsed arguments vanished along with my confidence. A cracked, "No!" was all I could muster. My lip trembled, so I bit down to keep from crying.

I glared at my brother. Why didn't he speak up? He'd been the one girly-crying in his sleep, and I'd promised to keep that a secret so Daddy wouldn't think less of him. But Will had turned his back, and busied himself with something or other in his tackle box. I supposed he'd be in on the grownup talk.

I looked back at Dad, dropped my fishing pole on the ground, and stomped away. About halfway up the hill, I yanked off my hat and threw it on the ground without missing a beat, then started pulling at the buckles of the life jacket.

"She'll be okay," I heard Mama say, "We'll take her to…" blah, blah, blah. The words were lost in the distance. I didn't need to hear. Their gifts—comic books, ice cream, or *whatever* —wouldn't fix this. Not *this* time. Maybe not *ever* again.

I got to our tent, yet didn't go in because it felt too small to hold my rage.

The buckles loose, I shrugged the lifejacket off my shoulders and let it drop to the ground. I stepped out of it, turned, and tried to stomp the life out of it. I kicked the lifejacket hard as I could and it flew into the tent.

What to do? I had to do something mean, maybe even cruel. Like pulling all the clothes hanging to dry from the line and dropping them in the dust. I could pour out their precious liquor. I could loosen the ties on the cots so they'd collapse or I could pull the tents down. Maybe I'd hide my egg salad sandwich in the hot car.

That idea seemed funny until I remembered I'd have a long ride home in that car too.

My eyes lit on Aunt Jewel's stash of cigarettes like they'd called out to me.

I didn't completely understand why, but I'd figured out how to get back at them.

Aunt Jewel must have forgotten to put the smokes away. The open carton lay upon the picnic table bench. I grabbed a pack, took a handful of strike-anywheres from the box on the table, and headed toward the playground where I'd seen that red-headed ape boy.

Sure enough, he was there, pushing what appeared to be his little brother on a swing. The sight of the small boy slowed my pace since I hadn't counted on having to babysit a snot-nosed brat. And as if on cue, the little one wiped his nose on the palm of his hand and rubbed the snot into his ratty red hair.

That cinched it—I changed course and headed back to our camp. I snagged one of Aunt Jewel's colas out of the cooler, and a chunk of ice to rub on my face and cool me down, though the cold did nothing for my anger. I downed the cola, plunked the bottle down onto the picnic table, and headed for the woods to spite my parents and *ruin everything.*

I followed a thin trail, more something animals would use. The path meandered in a way that told me I'd get lost, and that felt good. Soon enough, I found myself in the tall trees, where the air grew cooler and all I heard belonged to the forest.

A tree in a slight clearing stood out from the familiar pines and oaks. I didn't know what kind. The limbs dangled low, the leaves hanging from long tassel-like branches and forming a thin, uneven veil. I parted a section of the veil to pass under its canopy. Beneath, the roots spread out wide, like boney fingers gripping the soil. The space between two of them, padded with moss and lichen, looked like a cozy place to sit. The roots rose so high on either side of me that I knew I'd be hidden unless I chose to reveal myself.

The peaceful sounds all around eased the anger from me.

I considered the pack of cigarettes, but the thought of burning one of Aunt Jewel's stinky butts in that place turned my stomach. My thoughts of revenge, especially the one with the egg salad sandwich, seemed petty all of a sudden. Upsetting my parents wouldn't help my chances of going on the boat the next day.

The roots served as armrests. I settled in, savoring the *rightness* of being there *alone.* The soft moss on either side felt like a velvet cushion, more comfortable than the blue float. A great place for a nap, yet I knew I shouldn't remain too long, get too comfortable. I would stay in the woods a little while.

I closed my eyes, thinking about how I'd acted: Throwing down my fishing pole, stomping my life jacket, and stealing Aunt Jewel's cigarettes. I thought about how ugly I must have been, with my sulking, pouty face. The deafening buzz of my anger had left me; that droning, thought-killing whine that had filled my head. Though some anger lingered, I could at last think.

I decided I didn't want to be caught disobeying. I didn't want to *ruin everything.*

I *did* want to be on that boat on the lake tomorrow...

Opening my eyes, I saw my fingers tracing lazy patterns over the mossy, velvet skin of the roots. My hands stopped moving as if I'd caught them at something. I got that odd feeling again—that weird push-me-pull-me, like when I'd watched Aunt Jewel's lusty behavior down at the creek bank.

Feeling all-overish, I pressed my palms against the roots and pushed to shift my weight and find the most comfortable position. With little adjustment, I found a snug fit.

A few more minutes, I reminded myself. That feeling of belonging had returned, and my body didn't want to get up from that perfect spot. I felt less alone there than I did with my family. Again, shifting my shoulders, settling in, I felt the trunk at my back welcome me in an intimate sort of way. For a moment, I felt loved, protected, like I did sitting in Daddy's lap, resting my back against his chest.

But Daddy wasn't there, and the feeling turned. I wanted to rub all of me against the tree, and I became most aware of my backside and my bare thighs against the firmness under the moss. I liked the sensation. That brought shame.

And I sort of liked that too…

I stroked the giant root fingers, and a whispering came from overhead.

A breeze, rustling the leaves, I told myself.

A bit of cloud cover dimmed the light giving more of that sense of intimacy. With that, a new unease grew. Now, I felt *naked*.

What was I doing? Felt like I'd caught myself at something naughty. Why?

I looked to the surrounding trees. Oddly, now, they seemed to have their backs to me, for all the world like Will studying his shoes.

Another breeze blew through, a wetter one.

A prickling on the back of my neck.

A storm?

Time to leave.

I bent my knees and tried to shrug my way out because my arms were pinned at my sides. I shoved back with my elbows, and they got stuck.

Something *had* me!

Panicking, and twisting violently to get loose, I lunged forward, tearing the skin on my left arm as I came free and almost falling on my face.

Scrambling to my feet, I backed up to avoid leaves in my face. The veil, once a shelter from the outside, now moved wildly.

The temperature had dropped, the sky had darkened, and the wind picked up, tossing the long, thin branches like whips.

I turned back toward the tree to protect my face. Seeing what now looked like hips above the roots, I saw where I'd sat, a V-shaped cleft below a belly-ing out of the trunk. My eyes followed the bark upward. Knobs, where the loss of limbs had healed over, looked like a woman's bosom. To either side, limbs rose outward, with a diseased bulge between that glared at me through a bunch of knotty growths. Crows, clutching the limbs above, cussed at me with squawking voices.

"I'm sorry!" I shouted over the rising wind. The tree looked angry. Some-how, I'd upset her. I wanted to get away, but the threat of her whipping branches held me there. I thought she wanted to punish me. The leafy tassels struck my head, back, and shoulders, driving me back toward the trunk. One came at my face. I screamed and dodged, falling to the ground. Protecting my head, I held onto my glasses and rolled sideways until I'd passed beyond the veil, then got to my feet. In a few steps I'd be free, though I feared she might pull up her roots and come after me.

Shielding my face, I looked back. Her trunk did not move—she was like any other tree.

A cocky little monkey, I stood, hands on hips, and stuck my tongue out at her.

A flash, and a razor of pain as a whipping branch crossed my forehead and cheek. The lashing bowled me over. My glasses protected my eye. Clutch-ing my face with one hand, I used the other to help me crawl away across the ground. The squawking of the birds grew louder, and I feared they would dive at me. Two more lashes against my backside were a final spanking that got me to my feet. I ran blindly, bleeding into my hand, and crying out for help.

A low-hanging branch to my gut knocked the breath from me at the moment I saw through blood and tears the blurry, dark figure of a man in the distance, among the blowing trees. Stumbling back against a trunk, I choked, and finally gasped and coughed to restart my breathing. I couldn't see the man anymore or he had never been there. With air in my lungs, I ran, tripped over roots, lost a flipflop, got caught in vines and spun about.

I had to stop and look around, and I needed both eyes. I feared running into the man in the black fedora, since that is what the dark figure had be-come in my mind.

Pulling my hand away from my face, I saw blood all over the palm.

The forest danced in the wind, yet nothing came at me.

My breathing calmed some, I listened. Nothing but wind and moving trees. I'd got turned around, had no idea where I was, or how far I'd run.

Longer, deeper breaths.

What to do?

What would Daddy say?
No sun to guide me.
The water—where's the water?

The forest sloped downward to my right. The water would be there. I thought I could hear it, though the wind made a lot of noise.

I headed in that direction, found the creek, and moved along the bank upstream to the boat ramp. The wind, stronger near the water, and the deep rumble of thunder urged me on. Finally, I reached the ramp. Not a soul in sight. I turned onto the sandy path that led to the camp. My steps slowed, a trudge, a shuffle to the tent. I entered, fell onto my sky-blue float. While the rain drummed hard against the tent, I must have drifted off to sleep.

I floated in darkness on the ocean, face-down on my trusty float as chilly winds blew across my back. Seagulls cried, out of place in the night. But no, not gulls, voices, calling my name.

Lucy....

Luuuuuucyyyyyy...

"LUCY!"

Mama's voice, close: "Oh, thank God."

I tried to open my eyes. They wouldn't.

Daddy's voice, loud: "Hey, she's here! She beat us here! Must've been at the playground. Boy, howdy, that was a toad-strangler!"

Muted laughter answered. I heard someone enter the tent. Mama's hands gently rolled me over, and I half-opened one eye. Confused, I squinted blearily at her. Daddy crouched in the opening behind her.

Mama gasped. "Your eye!" She turned toward the more distant voices, said, "Someone get the first aid kit."

Daddy pushed in and lifted me into his arms. "There's blood on her arm." He lowered me onto a cot. He squatted and gave me my favorite smile. More awake now, I noticed his clothes were soaked through.

Mama turned my head away from Daddy so that she could tend to my cuts. I stared up at the tent's ceiling.

The running, the storm, the tree's anger. Had any of that really happened?

Mama tilted my head back, poured cold water over my cheek, dabbed at my face gingerly with a folded paper towel

When she pried my eyelid open, I cried out. That hurt, a lot!

Daddy's hand lit on my arm like a butterfly.

Mama covered my uninjured eye with the towel. "Can you see me?" she asked, leaning over me. Water dripped from her hair onto my neck. I nodded and reached toward my cheek.

"Don't touch it," she said.

I obeyed, but as she opened my eye again to wash the blood away with a squirt bottle from the kit, I gripped the cot frame against the sting and my feet danced.

"She's alright," she said over her shoulder. "Everyone out." Her no-nonsense voice was both commanding and reassuring. Everyone filed out of the tent.

Once we were alone, Mama turned back to me. "Let's get you cleaned up and in fresh clothes," she said.

~ ~ ~

The next morning had the kind of clean-washed splendor that follows a good blow. The storm had littered the camp with debris, mostly small pine branches with cones still attached, bits of paper, and overturned lawn chairs. On the lake, the air felt fresh and chilly. The world had righted itself, and I floated on the water in a boat with just Daddy for company, exactly as I'd wanted.

"What a morning!" he said, lifting his arms in an exaggerated stretch. "How you feelin', Rooster?"

"Great!" I said, lifting my own arms in imitation of his, then flapping them like wings.

He chuckled.

Much as I wanted to, I didn't truly feel great. I didn't feel *clean*. My thoughts had their own debris: fearful uneasiness about the tree, a weight of guilt for my misbehaviors, and a nagging sense that I'd seen and felt things I shouldn't have.

In my mind, I recalled the quiet moments alone in the tent with Mama. After cleaning me up, she had gingerly lifted my shirt over my head and checked my back for wounds. She tisked at a bruise across my ribs. Had been a long time since my mother helped me undress, and the act brought back a warm comfort I seemed to have forgotten. Suddenly, I craved a glass of milk. I took a sip of the water she offered instead and stood up so she could pull down my shorts.

Too late, I remembered the cigarettes. Her hand found the pack in my pocket, and her eyes got big.

I swallowed hard, bracing for what would come next.

Mama set the crumpled pack aside on the cot while she finished undressing me. When done, she rose and left the tent momentarily.

I froze, unable to take my eyes off the cigarettes as she stepped out of sight. Panic rose. Would she tell Daddy about the cigarettes?

To my relief, she returned alone, with fresh shorts, underwear, and a tee short. More importantly, she wore a warm smile. She placed the clothes on the cot beside the cigarettes, then made the crumpled pack vanish like a magician might have done. I know that couldn't be, but that *is* what I remember—the pack simply disappearing.

I sat back down, my legs wobbly again, and she knelt before me. She studied my injured eye.

"Thank you, Mama," I said.

She became still, and looked at me squarely. "You know, I think you *really* mean that."

Mama reached up and pressed her hand gently down on the top of my head, like she meant to hold me in that moment—whether for my benefit or hers, I couldn't tell.

"I want you to rest now," she said, and stood. "I'll get you something to eat." She paused before leaving. "I trust you'll tell your father about your adventure."

Mama had then left me wondering what she was up to. Somehow, I knew she looked out for me, and that Daddy would only know what I told him.

"This looks like a good spot," Daddy said, "let's try for some bream."

"Of course." I twisted around to grab my fishing pole.

"Try this one," he said. I turned back to see him lift a tarp and pull out a rod and reel, just my size—bright and shiny-new, and with a colorful lure already dangling.

"Wow!" I said, "…holy moly!"

He grinned.

I stood up carefully in the boat, planted my feet, and with a snap of my wrist, sank the lure about where I'd aimed.

"Now we're cookin'," he said, and sent his line out.

We settled into the comfortable quiet that came with fishing, a silence I loved. The one thing that might have made the outing better were *catawba* worms. In the spring, when they became available, Daddy used them for bait. He'd pick them off *catawba* tree leaves and place them on the cloth band of his straw hat. They wouldn't stray from the fabric. I loved watching them march endlessly around the band until he plucked them away one at a time to use as bait.

So many fishing trips with Daddy…I craved those moments of pure, quiet communion.

Yet I couldn't shake that uneasy feeling. Something had gone wrong. I didn't feel whole. The world around me didn't feel whole, and I wondered if things would ever be right again. What was missing?

My eyes kept looking hopefully to his hat band, even though I knew there weren't any of the caterpillars there.

He caught me looking once, twice, and the third time, I said, "Just thinking about those stupid *catawbas*." I looked away quick, feeling all-overish and not knowing why.

"Something wrong, Rooster?" He had a concerned look. "Some *thing* troubling you?"

I kept my head down and fiddled with my new rig. I knew his eyes remained on me.

Shame welled up out of nowhere. I felt heat on my face as a nameless guilt became a knot in my gut, too big for the silly crimes I'd committed.

What had I done wrong beyond stealing cigarettes and disobeying my parents?

What had happened under that tree?

I touched the bandage above my eye.

The tree had sure looked pissed off. Was that my fault? And what of the crows—I did see *them*. But *later*, with all the blood and tears blurring my vision... No, I couldn't be certain I'd seen the man in the black fedora.

I lifted my eyes to find Daddy still looking at me. "Rooster?" he said.

"I did something wrong in the woods—"

My line jerked.

"You got a nibble," Daddy said. "Be patient. It'll come back."

He looked to his own line, said quietly, "So what'd you do in the woods?"

"It's not what I did," I lied, having lost my nerve. "It's that I wasn't supposed to go there, and I stole a pack of Aunt Jewel's cigarettes to take with me."

Daddy chuckled, and I knew he didn't see the crime in what I'd done.

"That tree..." I began, not knowing what I'd say.

"What tree?"

"...Never mind," I said, feeling torn. How could I explain?

He chuckled again, and I should have felt relief.

I'd gotten away clean, but I still didn't *feel* clean. My confession incomplete, the knot in my gut tightened.

I looked toward the bank, scanning for the tree. Surely she stood close by. I could feel those knotty eyes watching me.

I might fool Daddy...

Another nibble, followed by a bite, and Daddy cautioned silently, holding out his hand. A strong pull told me the time had come to reel the fish in.

A fine bream, its silver scales flashing in the sun.

I told myself that all the bad feelings, and what I thought had happened with that tree were foolishness. The storm had upset me, and I'd lost my head. I told myself that I could think about all that on another day. That morning was for catching fish. In the evening, there would be the long ride home in the cool air. The car's vibration would lull me to sleep. And when I awoke, we'd be home and this whole week would become just one memory in a collection of others. I'd forget all about the scary part.

~ ~ ~

Spring, 1990

Driving home from a conference in Charleston, I saw the sign for Santee Cooper, and surprised myself by taking the exit and turning onto the two-lane road that led to the old fishing camp.

The farther I went, the more debris I saw on either side of the road. I recalled reading that Hurricane Hugo's storm surge had hit Santee Cooper hard. The camp's sign and the concrete bathrooms still stood. The little market had been obliterated and the area cleared. Farther in, the campsite would have been unrecognizable if not for a few concrete picnic tables and rusted old barrels. Most of the trees that had defined the area were either gone, broken, or limbless. The place looked small, and sad. I parked the car and got out, grateful for my sweater. No one in sight, but seeing tall stacks of trunks and limbs told me workers had been there clearing the downed trees recently. Chainsaws buzzed and cackled in the distance. Something about the row of wood stacks lining the water sparked an unease, vague until I remembered Will's nightmares of bonfires on the beach.

Back then, I'd thought Will's dreams stupid. I'd thought less of him for fearing them. After my experience with the tree, I'd had a new respect for the power of imagination to frighten. And I'd been way too hard on my brother. Hell, I'd been way too hard on my whole family.

I thought of my blue float and its smell rose up. More memories of that miserable August fishing trip came with it. Reliving that week and the pissy little girl I'd been, I turned away from the boat ramp and entered the woods without thought. A young girl with little control over her life, and adulthood looming in the not-too-distant future, I'd had a lot of formless fears back then. Had I projected them into the one place I'd always felt safe: the woods? Or had there been more to my frightening experience with the tree?

The hurricane had taken a ragged bite out of the shoreline where the creek opened into the lake, taking many of the pines away. I picked my way through the tangle of broken branches until I found what I must have been

115

looking for.

The tree had grown. This willow—as I now knew the tree to be—had become massive and she had held her ground, claiming the bank for herself alone. The long, dangling fronds hung limp and lifeless, though still green. The water began just beyond. Recollection hadn't put the tree so close to the creek. The surrounding trees had been reduced to broken sticks.

I approached on slightly higher ground. Most of the trunk was hidden by the curtain of twiggy limbs. The large roots were visible. I imagined those finger-like appendages digging in, grasping the shore as Hugo had tossed and blown through the area. My gut turned over, and a tightness gripped my throat, stopping me in my tracks. Unexpected tears blurred my vision.

I don't know how long I stood, frozen in place, torn between fascination and an urge to flee. The weeping willow of legend, mythology, and the occult stood before me. I'd been studying folklore in college. The conference I'd just left addressed the origins of local woodland folklore. The willow tree had come up a few times in the discussions; its link to the Moon and sorcery, the use of its twigs and bark for weaving and their medicinal properties, its ability to generate a new tree from a single twig stuck in the soil. None of what I'd learned suggested anything but a kindly form of life.

I longed to go down there, duck under the fronds and look up at that trunk. Yet, like a fish caught on a line, I resisted hard against the pull.

To this day, I tell myself that though the folklore is fascinating, I am not a believer. Even so, I always follow that thought with a knock on wood.

Had the willow whipped me because I hadn't shown due respect? Or had she done the loving thing, casting me out of my comfortable nest. The time had come for me to grow up, after all.

Looking at that lone, surviving tree, I knew I'd never have the answers to those questions.

The Outing
1971

Mama placed a pot of coffee on the table for Daddy, and turned to Will and me. "Finish up, and get ready. Ruth will be here soon. We have canning to do."

I stood at the sink as usual, rinsing my face after breakfast instead of using a napkin. I knew I wouldn't have time to brush my teeth.

"Yeah, hurry up, Lucy-fer," Will said, "I've got to get there early and give Jeff my notes for rehearsals."

Daddy dropped the paper and finished his coffee.

"Is that what you two were doing in the woods yesterday?" I giggled and covered my mouth. I thought they'd been practicing for a romantic scene and one of them had to be the stand-in for the girl. "Must have been gross."

Will's face went red and he stared at me. He looked sick, like he might puke. I turned to Daddy, thinking he might do something to help. His face had gone dark. He stared at Will from under his brow.

What had upset them?

Will's face turned white, and then I knew. He and Jeff weren't practicing for anything.

Daddy got up abruptly, his chair squealing loudly against the linoleum, and left the room. His keys jangled as he went out the back door, slamming it behind him. Will flinched at the sound.

He turned to me again, his face still frozen. We stared at each other in silence for the longest time.

What had I done? I had an inkling, but no real idea what that might mean for my brother and my father.

Finally, Will lowered his milk glass to the table slowly, and said, "Let's go."

He didn't speak to me or even glance my way the whole walk to school.

That afternoon when we got home, Mama was out running some errand

and Ruth had gone home.

Will called me into his room. I hoped he'd ask for my help with something. He sat at his worktable looking at me, his face stoney, until I asked, "What is it?"

He covered his mouth with a hand, and his eyes filled with worry. Once he moved the hand, I could tell he didn't want to say what was on his mind because he'd clamped his jaw shut and his lips had become a hard line.

Though I'd been a little afraid he'd get on me about what happened that morning, I could see that maybe for once, I had the upper hand. "What?" I asked, trying on some of the impatience he usually gave me.

"You—" he began and seemed to choke on the word.

I made as if to leave.

"Stop," he said.

I turned back, putting on a bored, vacant look, yet my hands had gone clammy.

"What you saw—Jeff and me, you weren't supposed to see that."

I'd thought about Will all day, and decided I shouldn't care what he did with his friend. That certainly wouldn't be the weirdest thing about him. I didn't see him differently because he might like boys.

"If anybody at school finds out..." he began.

Going into that with Will would only remind me that I'd betrayed him to Daddy. To avoid it, I blurted out "then maybe you shouldn't do it." I spun around and left his room, a cold thing to do, making my blunder even worse.

If only I'd told him that what I saw didn't matter to me, that it didn't change how I felt about him. Maybe if I had, things would not have gone so badly between us.

~ ~ ~

Seemed like no one in our household spoke to Will for the rest of the week. Of course, being holed up in his room working on projects didn't help, but that wasn't unusual for him. I might not have noticed the tension if I hadn't been the cause.

Friday night our parents went out to eat and see a movie. Will made ham and cheese omelets for us for dinner. We sat at the kitchen table to eat.

"I never told you what else I saw on the day that almost-dead baby came," Will said. "the one before you."

He set my dinner on the table before me, and sat to eat.

I knew he spoke of Mama's miscarriage.

He paused to pull a long, straight hair from his omelet. "One of yours, I think," he said, holding the pale strand up.

"I didn't get anywhere near the stove—" I began.

Will waved away my words, and brushed the hair off onto his pants.

"They didn't know what I knew," he said, "or, if they did, they didn't know I knew it too. I saw what Mama did." He fell silent.

I couldn't follow him. "What are you talking about?"

I started in on the omelet. Some of the egg didn't look done, the white part liquid and gross. I concentrated on the chunks of ham and the melted cheese.

He watched me, and I grew uneasy.

"Tell me," I said.

"Her belly was big and she had to struggle to climb onto the kitchen table. She stood up straight, and jumped right off. She didn't know I hid in shadows in the hall. I sat in the chair beside the grandfather clock and watched. I thought she was having one of her spells. Maybe I don't remember it right. I was pretty little. But I remember her face. She wasn't playing. She climbed up and jumped again, and again. She did it like ten times."

Will took a bite of his omelet. Then his face scrunched up like he'd remembered something really bad. "All of a sudden, I felt—I don't know—*wrong* sitting in that chair."

Penny's chair.

"I ran," he continued, "and hid under my bed until I heard Grandma and Ruth come in the house. Sounded like they were having a fight."

As I'd thought—probably the start of their falling out.

"I crawled out to see what was going on. Mama started screaming. They put her in bed and closed the door. They were still arguing, Ruth and Grandma. Annie Maude went out with the baby, and got in the car—I told you about that."

"You couldn't see who was driving, right?"

"Right." Will shook his head and his lips drew back from clenched teeth. "It's almost like a dream now. Maybe it was. For a while I'd try to ask Ruth about that day, but every time, she'd just give me a sweet or something to do."

"Why *would* Mama do that?" Like Will, I could only imagine she'd been having another one of her spells.

"Let me tell the rest, and then I'll say what I think."

I swear I saw pity for me in his eyes, briefly. That felt weird, and made me think he was up to something. He busied himself for a moment, cutting his omelet with his fork and taking a bite. Once he began to speak again, he didn't look at me.

"Later, when she was big with you, she did it again. She looked frightened when I came in the kitchen and caught her standing on the table. I don't know how many times she'd jumped before that. A little trickle of blood ran down her leg. I saw that."

Will glanced at me, and I could tell he knew I had become uneasy with what I'd heard. He had the slightest smile, and began to speak more rapidly, maybe to tell the rest before I got up and left. Yet what he had to say, something I'd never heard before, involved *me*. I wasn't going anywhere.

"She got off the table, saying something I couldn't understand. I called Daddy at work and told him about it. He and Annie Maude were at the house minutes later. I remember Daddy grabbing me and hauling me out of the house. I thought *I'd* done something wrong and he was going to punish me, but we got in his car and went fishing. When we got back, Mama was in bed. She stayed there until you were born."

No longer did he have to tell me what he thought Mama had been doing. I'd figured the truth out for myself, though I sure didn't want to look squarely at it. His story explained a lot about that look Mama gave me every so often. I didn't *just* stand in her way, I was unwanted.

She'd killed Penny and tried to kill me too!

And Grandma *knew*!

He glanced at me again. His ever-so-slight smile disappeared suddenly and he got the worried look of someone who knew he'd taken something too far. But he hadn't finished—no, he had to double-down on his cruelty so I would believe he'd meant to go that far all along. A guy thing to save face, I guess. He shrugged like he'd been talking about nothing special and his condescending attitude returned. Then he delivered what he no doubt thought of as a punchline—more like a punch to my gut. "I suppose I saved your life, showing up like that unexpected."

My memory of picking up the fork is missing. The next thing I knew, I'd hurled the utensil at him. I had aimed for his right eye. Thankfully, the tines pierced his left cheek instead. He hollered, and pushed back from the table, almost falling over with his chair. The fork went flying.

"Y-you'd better stay away from me," he stammered, stumbling back and fleeing to his room.

My automatic reaction had seriously frightened me too. Lucky I'd missed!

I went to my room and buried my face in my pillow, weeping. I held my lucky penny and tried to remember all the good times I'd had with Daddy. That took the sharpest edge off the pain. *He* surely loved his Rooster.

Eventually, my thoughts turned to the times Mama had looked upon me with genuine warmth. I remembered the fear in her eyes on a rainy night by the side of the road, and her relief upon learning I hadn't been harmed. She'd been beautiful in that moment, and I'd felt loved.

At nine years old, shortly after Grandma gave me my cabinet, I'd torn from a catalog a picture of fancy wingtips like those worn by the man in the black fedora. Using that as my object, I'd tried to tuck the memory of that event away in my cabinet. When the attempt failed, I'd tried again with the same results. I could not rid myself of memories of the man, and I couldn't bring myself to ask Annie Maude what I'd done wrong.

If the effort had paid off, I might have also been putting away that moment of Mama's love.

Though early in the evening still, with full dark around the corner, I'd exhausted myself. I turned on my side, pulled the bed sheet over me, and slept.

~ ~ ~

Sunday morning at breakfast, when Mama and Daddy first saw the scabs on Will's cheek, I thought I'd be grounded or worse.

"How'd that happen?" Mama asked.

Will glanced at me so quickly, I may have been the only one to notice. "I was running through the woods with a friend yesterday, and he let a branch snap back at me. He didn't mean to." Again, he glanced at me.

"Who was the friend?" Daddy asked, his voice cold.

Will turned white again, said quietly, "Ian."

"That is a soft-sounding name," Daddy said. "Think twice about hanging around boys like that." He pushed back from the table, got up, and left the kitchen.

"You boys are just too wild in those woods, like animals," Mama said, shaking her head and wringing her hands.

With Daddy gone from the room, some of the color returned to Will's face. He glanced at me without anger.

I mouthed silently, "I'm sorry," hoping he could read my lips,

"Me too," he mouthed back.

Will wasn't such an ass, after all. He'd taken the punishment I'd doled out for his intentional cruelty, and perhaps he understood that I didn't mean to expose his secret to Daddy. I didn't feel good about what I'd done with the fork, but decided maybe we were even.

A lot of good that did me. I still had a weight on my heart from what he'd told me, something I didn't want to carry around. Annie Maude had given me a way to deal with that. I had to figure out what object I'd use to represent the memory.

Mama
1971

The more I thought about what I'd learned from Will about Mama and me, the more I saw Penny as bound up in it. When Mama looked at me, she must have seen Penny too. While I believe Mama did love me, those feelings must have come with some pain.

I told Grandma all about my visits from Penny and what I'd learned from Will. Telling what I knew and watching her, I saw that she'd suffered from the same knowledge, and that she had for a lot longer.

Like my brother, when asked about who drove the car that took her and the infant away that day, Annie Maude said, "I can't say."

I thought she could, yet pressing her for a better answer would get me nowhere.

"I want to put it in a jar and be rid of it," I said. "I've tried to come up with a simple proviso to allow me to remember Penny but forget what Mama did. It's hard. Can you help?"

"What your mother did so defines who Penny is, I don't think you can rid yourself of the bad memories without losing her. Because she's at the heart of it, whatever you put in that jar should come from Penny. Once the jar is put away, you won't know her at all, except once a year when you examine what's in the cabinet. Those brief periods of her will have to be enough."

That was for the best, I decided. Bunny's button eye, the one I'd found on the chair after giving the stuffed animal to Penny, would be the object used. We placed it in a white jar and buried that in the small plot Grandma had given over to me in her garden. I hoped that at least Penny approved of the delphiniums and columbine I planted above the burial.

And sure enough, in the following weeks, the house went quiet, along with the recollections. Of course, I only became aware of that upon digging up the jar a month later to put it in my little red cabinet. Again, awareness of Penny lingered a short time before fading.

Before I put the jar in the cabinet, Annie Maude had placed an arm around me. "Of all that you've put away," she said, "this memory is by far the most important to look at each year. Knowing you as I do, I believe you'll resist looking at it. I'll make certain you do, come next birthday, but I won't always be here. There will come a time when you have to do it all by yourself. Your poor sister is involved. She communicates with you for her own reasons, perhaps because Penny simply needs family. You have grown frightened of her, but you've also said that at first you wanted to play with her. I suggest you try to find a place for her in your heart."

At that age, I didn't want to think about having to love someone I didn't already have feelings for, especially since the someone in question was a pale, creepy creature that made my skin crawl. I hadn't been able to eat egg since Will told me about that trickle of blood. I'd hardly been able to look at Mama.

"Sure," I said.

She knew better. "Sweetheart, I agreed to help you set aside that memory because I can see how much it hurts. Yet, another life, a very short one, is involved. You must allow for that. Penny is still with us in ways that none of us can truly understand. Your mother doesn't want to consider that the lost child might have needs. She has never believed in what I do, and I don't mean she just doesn't think much of it."

"Why do I have to be the one to do something about it? Penny is—"

"Because you may be all she'll ever have. At the time you mother lost Penny—"

"You mean when she *killed* her," I said coldly.

"…and admitted to me what she'd done," Annie Maude continued, "I tried to help her make amends to that child, but she wouldn't have any of it. I suggested she find some way to talk to you about it with the hope that that would draw you two closer and help heal her wound. Instead she has chosen to carry the regret all these years. She tells me how much it weighs on her. She's penitent within herself, but she knows the shame of what she did has kept you two apart. I'm afraid that one day it might bring much worse. Once, when you were a toddler, she took a whole bottle of pills. Thankfully, your father came home in time or we might have lost her. After she'd recovered, Suzanna admitted to me she'd taken the pills because she could no longer bear her regrets over what she'd done."

Using the word "lost" like that always bothered me. I concentrated on that triviality rather than listening because I didn't want to be responsible in any way for Penny.

"Do you understand?" Grandma asked.

Nodding dutifully, I set the jar down on the shelf next to others like it, and shut the door.

~ ~ ~

In late September, Mama, closing in on middle-age, yet beautiful and physically healthy, walked down the back steps with a basket of laundry to hang in the sunshine on a lovely, sunny morning. Ruth said Mama had pinned up the towels and underpants and put the extra pins back in the cut-away Clorox bottle hanging from the line. She'd put the basket on the steps of her pristine, screened-in porch. Then she must have turned and walked down to the Savannah River. Stepping in, she'd given herself to the water, and left us behind.

Crows had come in great numbers that day.

She should never have spoken to *him*.

And what about me? I'd spoken to him too.

Her body was discovered washed up against one of the pilings of the railroad trestle. That cast a pall over my friend, the river. Afraid, I'd somehow catch her ghost, I never fished that spot again.

I thought Mama had taken her own life because of her mental illness. I didn't remember her jumping off the kitchen table, I didn't remember Penny, and the two of us being unwanted children. I didn't even remember Annie Maude telling me that Mama's regrets had made her suicidal once before.

The funeral took place on a Saturday. Standing in the cemetery, and later, at the reception, I felt apart from everyone. So many had gathered to hear words that had no impact on me—I'd grown numb. I suffered through a lot of standing around and waiting, trying not to make eye contact with anyone, including the people I cared most about, even Chet. At the reception, that became all the more important because it could draw sympathy from people I barely knew or didn't know at all. And I sure as hell didn't want to talk to *them*. Everyone had dressed up for the occasion, and the smell of cologne and perfume in the air had my stomach roiling. I tried not to breathe, as I looked for a spot to escape the stupid, pumped-in organ music—I never found one.

Of the things said to me that day, one made me smile. My second cousin, Pearl Higginbotham, told me. "Your mama and me, we used to go to dances together when we were young. She was the life of the party. All the boys want-ed to dance with Suzanna."

I had trouble imagining that until I pictured the beautiful woman hug-ging me by the side of the road in the rain.

Annie Maude spoke to me briefly at the reception. "You should not wait to consider your stowed memories. There is one jar in particular having to do with your mama that you should open right away. If you don't want to walk to my house, I can come get you."

I didn't want to think about *those things*. I'd put them away for a reason.

~ ~ ~

Some of Daddy's cold silence toward my brother had lifted a few days after I'd betrayed Will's secret. With Mama's death, the coldness returned. Daddy was anything but quiet about his anger.

The morning following the funeral, Daddy told Will, "You'll take over your mother's duties around the house, cooking and cleaning in your spare time before and after school on the days Ruth isn't here."

I thought that if Helen had still been living with us, he might have asked her to help out too, Then Daddy made it clear that he meant it as punishment, saying, "That kind of work shouldn't be too hard for someone of your sort." He looked away, and I could see he regretted his words. Yet, like Will had done with me, he had to show he'd really meant it. "Your mother was ashamed of you."

Tears threatening to spill, Will said, "At least she loved my *real* father."

Daddy looked as if he'd been slapped. I'd never seen him act like such an ass before. He had a look I didn't recognize. I had the weirdest thought that maybe I'd awakened in the wrong house, in some other family. Although all else looked familiar, the home I'd always known suddenly felt dry and fragile, ready to go up in smoke if a match were lit.

"Daddy," I started, not knowing what I'd say, needing to defend Will somehow.

"Not now," he said.

I tried to talk to him a while later. He shushed me, said, "I know, but I won't talk about it."

He wrote up a schedule of duties for Will, which included two days a week when he'd run Daddy to work so he'd have the car to do the shopping. "It'll be up to you to get your sister to help you," he said.

Ruth came on Monday.

"Daddy blames Will for Mama's death," I told her. I chose not to say he thought his son a sissy.

"You just do your best to help your brother," she said. "That boy has always been a bit sensitive. That's why he close himself off from the rest of us. Your father's a good man. Once he don't hurt so bad, he'll see the error of his ways."

I'd never thought of Will as sensitive. I could see it, once she'd said that.

Ruth kept a list of everything we ran low on so Will would know what to get at the store.

Feeling sorry for him, I worked extra hard to help where I could, doing the dishes, taking the garbage out, sweeping, and such.

Home from work and hungry, Daddy made a big scene Wednesday night, shouting and stomping about. "I can't eat eggs every meal," he said, then threw a bowl of scrambled eggs against the wall and stormed out.

I don't know what he had to eat that night. Will and I had chicken noodle soup from a can and ketchup sandwiches.

Ruth shared a few simple recipes with Will the next day.

Annie Maude came to take me to her house for the weekend. I didn't want to leave Will alone, but she insisted. We rode in her old, blue Packard that smelled of lilacs and leather. At her house, she again encouraged me to consider my stored memories.

I shrugged and turned away.

"You must not wait," she said, turning me back.

"In the morning."

She nodded.

~ ~ ~

I took the crooked, squeaky steps to the cellar slowly, in no hurry to visit the burdens I'd put away. Light streamed in through the dingy windows, catching on cobwebs and illuminating my red cabinet. Opening its doors, I saw the silhouette of Bunny's button eye through the milky white glass, and the memories tickled at the back of my mind. I opened the few jars that held items. The recollections seeped in as I stood there. When done, I was amazed to see how far the light had shifted across the floor. Having decided that memories of Penny would be the last I'd want to recall each year, I pushed her jar, with the bunny eye, toward the empty ones at the rear of the cabinet. In that moment, I knew I'd be happy to never recall any of it ever again.

I climbed the stairs to find Annie Maude's warm embrace. She pushed the hair out of my eyes and I forced a smile. "There's my girl," she said.

"I shouldn't stay. I have to go home and have a talk with Daddy right away, before the memories fade."

"Stay for lunch and let's talk about your mother, then I'll drive you home."

We had sardines on Saltine crackers with yellow mustard, a favorite since she'd first prepared that lunch for me. I liked that I would willingly eat the whole fish, except for its head, bones and all. Not many children I knew, especially girls, would be willing to do that.

With a few tears, we spoke of Mama, recalling pleasant memories. I even told a story that made us laugh, one about a snake in the garden scaring her.

"When Daddy caught it in a shoebox and she saw how tiny it was, she pretended to be frightened again, and laughed herself silly. I don't know why she named the snake, but she did. Ever after that, all snakes in the garden were Clyde. If we heard a squeal from the garden while Mama was out there, one of us, me, Will, or Daddy would say, 'Clyde's back!'"

Annie Maude and I had a good laugh over that.

~ ~ ~

At home, I found Will watching some science show on PBS. He had a big bruise on his cheek and a smaller one on his forehead. Annie Maude had already driven away, or I would've had her come in to see what I'd discovered.

"Daddy's in bed, passed out," Will said. He put a hand to the bruise. "This was last night. He went out after that, and came back sometime in the night. He's been in bed since."

"What happened?"

"I hit *him* first," Will shook his head. "It doesn't matter. He hates me. He finds a reason to mistreat me no matter what I do."

"I'm sorry."

"I know it's not your fault."

"That's not what I mean and you know it."

He nodded.

I went in to see Daddy. He smelled of liquor, and that made me think of the fishing trips with aunts and uncles, all the drinking they did, their slurred words, and the loose talk they made when liquored up. Disgusted, I left him, and sat with Will on the couch.

"Drunk," I said.

"Yeah, no shit…"

"So…" I said slowly, hoping Will would think about why.

"Yeah, so what?"

"So *maybe* it's 'cause he feels bad about what he did."

"Good. Let him lose a precious day off, *sleeping* it off."

I couldn't blame him for being angry. Still, I had to talk to Daddy. "Do you know how to make coffee?"

"Yeah, but I'm not making coffee for *him*. I'm not doing anything for him I don't have to."

"Yes, you are." I took him by the hand and pulled him into the kitchen.

"Okay," he said with a sigh. "I'll make a pot, and then I'm leaving while he sobers up."

"Good."

~ ~ ~

"Daddy," I said too quietly. Then louder, "*Daddy, wake up.*" He lay on his side, his face turned toward the mattress and a pillow scrunched up against the side of his head. I pulled the pillow out of the way, and shook him by the shoulder. He groaned and swatted uselessly at the air with his left hand.

"Your Rooster is crowing," I said, "Time to wake up, Daddy!"

"Go away," he mumbled.

"No, I have coffee for you. You have to get up and talk to me. Something *terrible* has happened."

He rolled onto his back, eyes closed, and said, "What happened?"

"My mama is gone," I said, my voice cracking, "and my daddy is beating up my brother." And without wanting to, I began to cry. "I don't know what to do." I barely got the words out. Leaning into his shoulder, I hugged him the best I could, though he stank of liquor and sleep.

He put his arm around me. I saw through a blur of tears that he'd opened a squinty eye. "Rooster, I'm sorry. I've hardly even looked at you since your mother…"

"I don't care about that!" I sat up. "You have to get out of bed and talk to me. *Right now.*"

"Oh, honey, I had a hard night."

I slapped his shoulder hard. "No, you *didn't*," I yelled, "you got *drunk*."

The one other time I'd raised my voice with Daddy we'd been fishing, and he'd accidentally stuck me with his fishhook twice, so I didn't know how he'd take it. My words or my hand must have stung, because both his eyes had popped open. He propped himself up with an arm. "What's going on here?" he said like he'd just awakened.

I rolled off the bed and stood. "There's coffee on your nightstand. Get up and come to the kitchen and talk to me. Bring that coffee and drink it so you'll sober up." I couldn't believe I'd given my father commands. Even so, he was full of shit and would hear about that from his thirteen-year-old.

I left the room, figuring he had no choice but to do as I said. My anger made me feel that kind of powerful.

And when he came ambling into the kitchen, carrying his coffee cup, I must've thought I could do anything. "Sit down," I commanded. I set the coffee pot and an ashtray on the table.

He stood, rubbing his head with a pained look. "Please, Rooster, don't shout. I have a terrible headache."

"Good," I said. "You deserve it."

He'd gone to bed in the clothes he'd worn the day before. They were a wrinkled mess. He had a shoe on one foot, the other had a sock, hanging half off. I'd never seen Daddy so low, with all sense of dignity gone. Seeing that, my anger vanished and I grew upset, even a bit frightened. What if he stayed that way? What if he became a drunk? While he fished in his shirt pocket for his cigarettes and matches, I wiped away fresh tears with a napkin.

Daddy sat heavily in the chair opposite me at the kitchen table. He moved the ashtray so he could reach it more easily, lit a cigarette, and sipped his coffee.

"You hit Will," I whispered.

"Yes, I did," he said after a moment, without looking at me. Then he covered his face with a hand.

"Should you apologize to him?"

He seemed to struggle with that. My anger began to rise again.

"Worried you'd look *weak*?" I asked.

"You can't talk to me like that," he said, his voice powerless, muffled by his hand. He wouldn't look at me.

"I heard from Annie Maude that Mama tried to kill herself once before, with pills."

"Yes."

"Did Mama tell you it was because she regretted what she'd done to Penny, and tried to do to *me*?"

Daddy looked up at me, his eyes narrowing. "Penny?" He shook his head. "...No." He blinked hard several times. "What did your mother do to you?"

I smacked my open hand onto the tabletop and he winced at the sharp sound.

"That's enough—" he started with a stern look.

I interrupted him. "Do you remember her jumping off this table when she was big with me?"

He clearly didn't want to answer. "There's no need to—"

"*Do you?*" I shouted.

He gave in and nodded. "But, sweetie, you shouldn't—"

"Did you know she did it with Penny too, but there wasn't anyone to stop her that time? Will saw her, and told me about it. Remember when Mama took that whole bottle of pills? Grandma said Mama told her she'd done that because she couldn't live with what she'd done to Penny and nearly did to me. Annie Maude says she's certain that's why Mama killed herself."

Daddy stared at me with his mouth open, a hurt look slowly taking hold of him. His eyes shifted to focus beyond the window, with the look of someone thinking about the past. His cigarette fell from his fingers. He picked it up off the table, and snuffed it out in the ashtray.

"So, Mama didn't kill herself because she was ashamed of Will," I said. "It had more to do with me than him. Please don't mistreat him anymore. We've always known he's not like everybody else."

Daddy buried his face in his hands and sobbed.

Unlike his other recent outbursts, that one didn't frighten me. I got the feeling he'd had a change of heart, one that would help Will.

I got up to make scrambled eggs for us both, my hands shaking. The eggs didn't gross me out that time. Tired of them or not, he had no complaints.

Will came home later, and Daddy said to him, "Let's go for a ride."

Hours passed before they returned. When they did, they were laughing about something.

I never asked what was so funny.

~ ~ ~

Annie Maude died in her sleep in late summer of 1972. I missed her like nobody's business, and regretted not spending more time with her than I had. Without her guidance and reminders, I made a lot more mistakes, not the least of them having to do with my cabinet. Nobody could tell me what happened to her cabinet. Ruth got Mr. Johnson to haul mine from Grandma's cellar to our house, where it took up a neglected corner in the shed out back.

Something October
1997

October doesn't come to the California desert. The month starts with good intentions in the Northeast, maybe in Maine, works its way west and south, but turns tail somewhere in Oklahoma or West Texas, a little before its first good taste of desert and long before the parched cities of southern California.

Living in the desert since 1992, I'd missed it. October isn't just a month for me, it's a state of mind.

Today, though, October had nearly passed me by. November would begin next week. I was hurrying to the Post Office before it closed. My back hurt, so I scrunched into the seat in search of a more comfortable position, driving one-handed with the windows down. The dry air whipped my hair back and forth across my sunglasses—which somehow maintained a film of dust—while Bad Religion shook the rearview mirror.

I'd just left the foundry with a new bronze packed in its box in the back seat. A carnival contortionist, male in form, dressed in tight jester's motley. I'd bent the figure like a nightmare pretzel, with a faint hint of facial features and deep hollows for eyes. I hadn't wanted to do the sculpture, yet bronze-level money was hard to turn down. The piece should have shipped two weeks earlier, but I'd dragged my feet.

I popped both "up" buttons—a reflex learned quickly in the desert—to close the windows against a curtain of sand ahead. The windshield bore the pitted signatures of previous sandstorms—an unpleasant aspect of the desert. More and more I asked myself why the hell I stayed there.

Unlike the cruel wind in the desert, the autumn breezes in the East felt like promises, carrying colorful leaves and the rich, loamy scent of change. Growing up with a birthday on October 5th, I seemed to turn each year with the leaves, and not just older. With another year, had I grown taller? Probably. Prettier? Maybe. Were my eyeglasses thicker? Yes—*sigh*. Was I smarter? *Was* I smarter?

With each new carpet of leaves, I assessed what another year had brought me.

Of all that mattered in my childhood and all that didn't, October had consistently brought a particular magic: The County Fair.

At fourteen years of age, I saw the contortionist. More importantly, he saw me.

On the evening of what had been a damp, chilly South Carolina day in the fall of 1972, Daddy and I walked about the annual county fair. Chet would be going with his brothers. I'd become distant from my friend since Mama died. Besides, he had grown tall, and had a proper girlfriend. Pretty and talented, she played the piano at church, her blonde hair in tidy curls. Daddy and I spent the afternoon among strange, but familiar sights, sounds, and smells, a much-needed break from our lingering grief. We'd seen the craft shows, livestock, and jars of pickles wearing blue ribbons. We'd had the corndogs you can only get at carnivals, saw Joeys hawking their crooked games, heard the steam-powered carousel music, and smelled the vinegar fries, served up in greasy paper cones. We got dizzy on the Octopus, staggered through the Tilt House, picked our way through the House of Mirrors, and rode the Ferris wheel to get a great view of the river.

Mama would have hated being at the carnival, and would have made that known. Even so, I'd have given anything to have her with us.

By dusk, my feet were dragging. Still, as we neared the exit, coming upon the last tent on the midway, I wanted more. Through its opening, I made out a wooden stage with a skirt in need of repair and a black drapery backdrop, perfect for displaying the "Strange Attractions" promised on the sign above the entrance. A tall, thin man out front drawled on about the curiosities inside, not even pausing when he took our tickets with his skinny, red-stained fingers. He stuffed them in the pocket of his ratty jacket. We stepped solemnly into the darkness within and stood in the sawdust near the stage. A well-known waltz, poorly arranged, played from hidden speakers, the sound tinny, and cheap. The few others gathered there seemed restless for the show to continue.

A man standing next to Daddy said, "You just missed Lady Lamia. She wasn't very convincing."

Daddy smiled.

Someone closed the tent flap and quickly the air grew stuffy. I became too aware of time passing while waiting in the darkness.

Finally, the music stopped. Following a short silence, a fanfare blared. A spotlight washed over the stage, and a performer burst from between the musty folds of the curtain. He looked a lot like the fellow out front who had taken our tickets. Long and wiry, he wore a black leotard and white makeup on his entire head and neck. He bent so far backwards as to "birth" his head and arms from between his knees, then skittered spider-like to the center of the stage.

Everyone gasped.

My mind's label maker punched the letters, B-E-N-D-Y-M-A-N.

He crept to the edge, a mere yard from where I stood.

Though too old for such a thing, I slipped my hand into Daddy's larger one, regretting that last candy apple.

Bendyman's pink-rimmed eyes, like wounds against the white, slowly surveyed the audience. Fearing those eyes might find me, I felt terribly small, yet not small enough.

Mask, mask, mask it, elastic, basket.

The nonsense words escaped me in whispers. That was the first time I'd used such rhymes to calm myself.

Thank you, Deb, my weirdo angel.

I couldn't help remembering Mama talking to Aunt Aldean about it, "No, no, it's not a tic. It's a habit—from a *game* she plays with her friend, Debbie, next door. She'll outgrow it."

And that led to thinking about Mama's death in the Savannah River. *Savannah, savannah, banana, yummy savannah, have some, Suzanna. Good to the last drop.*

I squeezed Daddy's hand and looked up at his chin. He nodded to the music and took a drag off his smoke. The chin bobbed up and down, the cigarette with it, flaring red.

The contortionist stood on one leg, reached behind him with the other leg, and scratched the back of his head with a toe.

His eyes found me!

My vision grew a little black at the edges. I rocked gently back and forth. *His face. His face his face's face, amazing grace, erase this place.*

My finger's dug into the solid, familiar hand. Daddy looked at me somewhat surprised, perhaps because I had slowly withdrawn from everyone, huddled into myself, after Mama died. I couldn't remember the last time I'd touched anybody, even Ruth.

The moment stretched and thinned. The sawdust smell became overwhelming. Laughter from the audience sounded damp. The music faded away. I stood on rubber.

And then, a terrible thing—Bendyman spoke directly to me, his face somehow inches from mine. "Well, hello there. Remember me?" The last two words seemed to be a command rather than a question.

And a worse thing—he grinned at me a mouth full of gold teeth. He *did* seem familiar. And not just from taking our tickets.

My legs turned to spaghetti. I sagged to the floor—a terrible sinking spell—sawdust grinding into my knees.

Time snapped back into place at last. The music returned, and Daddy's cigarette again bobbed with his head.

Somehow, I'd gained my feet. Scratchy sawdust clung to my knees. I stood next to Daddy. My hand had mysteriously found his again.

The show had ended. Bendyman was nowhere to be seen. Two clowns and an ancient poodle were exiting through the drapery at the back of the stage to a smattering of applause. How long had we been standing there? We followed the others, shuffling through the tent flap, out into the glare of the midway lights.

The barker had resumed hawking the tent-show. He greeted us as we passed. "Well now, hello again," he said, and with a flourish, handed me a free ticket to The Monster House. I looked up at him. He wore a porkpie hat, and traces of the white makeup still defined his jawline. The contortionist I'd seen performing, Bendyman, and this sinewy fellow were indeed one and the same. How had he gotten out there so fast? Had I lost more time than I'd thought?

With the makeup mostly wiped off, I saw a fancy number seven tattooed on his neck. Then I recognized that grin full of gold teeth. Bendyman was *also* Pretzel, the convict Chet and I had seen working at the bakery in town on that summer day so long ago. He'd shown that grin when he'd frightened us away from the cellar window. Of course, a convict would take what work he could get, but he also had a talent.

Feeling self-conscious, and ashamed of my weird, weenie reaction to the sideshow performance, I murmured a quick thanks, snatched the ticket, and ran back up the midway to the ride. My mood lifted as I neared The Monster House—my favorite—one of those "couples" rides in the dark, with lame jump-scares that got arms around shoulders and kisses in the dark.

That had been over twenty years earlier. These memories had come up because of a coincidence: My most recent bronze creation being a contortionist, and seeing an actual living contortionist the day before. The man had been one of many buskers drawn to the city during the date palm festival. Though he seemed too old for that sort of work, he still had some moves. Possibly another coincidence, he'd had an elaborate number seven tattooed on his neck, just like the convict, Pretzel. Weird, yet no way he could be the same man. I decided that the number seven might be some carnie thing having to do with contortionists.

Still contemplating that evening with Daddy at the carnival, I realized my recollection didn't include actually taking the ride in The Monster House.

The last thing I remembered was riding home with Daddy, sitting on the cold seat, my head on his shoulder, while I wept inconsolably.

"I know, Rooster," he'd said, "we've lost too many loved ones."

Daddy died in a car accident about a week later. His car went over the embankment into the Savannah River. He'd been all dressed up in his Sunday best, even though it happened on a Wednesday.

Helen got a job at the local hospital and moved back home to live with Will and me.

My thoughts too morbid, I needed relief. To the beat of "Stranger than Fiction," I ticked off Joshua trees as I passed them along the highway. Being desert trees, their leaves didn't make warm colors and drop to the ground in fall. They merely became gray and dull.

Nope! I lived in the desert, now. October was a no-show.

I arrived to find a nearly empty lot at the post office. Inside, no one stood in line and I concluded my business quickly, feeling fortunate that I didn't have to stand waiting with a sore back. Leaving, postal receipt in hand, I enjoyed the brief sense of closure that came with shipping an art order.

Then I saw my car. At least ten crows had perched on the roof and hood. I pressed the key fob to unlock the doors, and the crows all took flight at once with a great noise of wings and scattering of loose feathers. Distracted by a bit of black down falling near my face, I missed seeing the crow shit on my door handle and put a hand in it.

Back home, in the kitchen, the coffee maker's red light glowed. *Good!* I grabbed a cup from the cupboard, but froze as I reached for the pot of coffee.

My hand puppet. The toy had long, stringy arms and legs that could be tied in knots—another contortionist! I'd never thought of that before. I kept the puppet in a small glass case in my studio. Had I forgotten getting it out and placing it there?

I'd found the puppet tucked away in a shoebox with old photos in 1992, the same year I'd moved to the desert. I had briefly returned to South Carolina to help Helen sort the house in preparation for selling it. Excited, I'd carried it into the next room to show her.

"Yes," she said, "you got that puppet when you were in the hospital, didn't you?"

"Yes, pneumonia."

"I'm tired of crying, Let's not talk about that."

We were both tired, having suffered through the clearing effort with bouts of tears and regrets over things left unsaid, , even though Mama and Daddy

135

had already been gone for many years.

And where the hell was Will? Helen had probably summed up his excuses quite well when she'd said, "He thinks he's got better things to do."

I chose to believe that coming to help would have been too painful for him.

Looking at her watch, she said, "The morning's gone by so fast. Got to go, but I'll be back in time to get you to the airport." And she'd left the house.

I had been delighted to find the puppet because it represented my survival of pneumonia, a badge of sorts. Yet there had always been something frightening about it as well, something I'd always thought reasonable and tolerable considering the difficult illness in which I'd acquired the toy.

Finishing up at Daddy's house, I went out to the shed to see if anything there might be worth saving. The little red cabinet sat where it had since shortly after Annie Maude's death, its condition a mystery under a thick blanket of dust and cobwebs. Deciding that too much effort would be required to pack and ship the piece of furniture across the country to my place in the desert, I considered cleaning it out so whoever bought Daddy's house wouldn't have to sort through the odd contents. Fearing what memories might be conjured in the process, I turned away and left the shed.

I had stopped revisiting them once a year like Grandma had instructed me to do, reasoning that Annie Maude had taught me all that foolishness to help me cope with the tough parts of my young life. Lesson learned, I'd decided, figuring grownups didn't need such fanciful devices to manage fears, regrets, hopes, and dreams. Adults simply swallowed them and washed the shit down with a glass of denial.

I had put the puppet back in its shoebox full of old photos and stowed that in my suitcase for my return flight to the desert. Once home, I'd had the urge to seal the puppet up somewhere, whether to keep the toy safe or keep me safe from it, I couldn't say. That's how the little guy ended up in its own display case in my studio.

I had a spacious apartment, with a huge, well-lit room for working, and private balconies off the bedrooms. That stretch of desert has one good point: The sun goes down early behind the mountains to the west and the skies are incredibly clear, the sunsets spectacular. I stood on the balcony, finishing my coffee, watching as the stars peeked through the deep blue of the retreating day. Not wanting to shut myself in, I considered making a bed on the balcony in the company of the stars. I often camped there, but dust storms were in the forecast. Reluctantly, I returned to my isolation, the cocoon I'd created.

Increasingly over the last few years, I'd wondered why I had come to the desert. I didn't like the place much. What had made me run from home and all I'd known my entire life?

The only answer available was that I felt haunted, without knowing what pursued me or why. I'd been plagued with nightmares my entire adult life. I'd been in therapy, taken depression medication, wasted a year on a self-help course on inner peace and hope, and smoked an awful lot of dope.

Finally, when I'd begun my art career, I'd settled on living with them. I'd sculpted them and those nightmares had brought me success. Recently, I'd completed the project of a lifetime for a gallery show at the Big Horn Pavilion during the Date Palm Festival: A miniature carnival inspired by the October fairs I'd explored in childhood—a midway, with rides and sideshows. My way of bringing at least a hint of fall's magic to the desert. I employed the latest in computer technology to give the exhibit magic in the form of light and motion, sounds and smells.

Using my nightmares as a source for my art, I'd turned lemons into lemonade. I'd reveled in the dark and disturbing. Recently though, that haunted feeling had become stronger, and I wondered if building that carnival had been a good idea, after all. Homesickness kept telling me something had been misplaced in my past and ought to be found.

Following my mother's death, Annie Maude's, and then my father's the following year, undefinable guilt had grown over me like a thicket of kudzu, walling me off from others while I reshaped my memories and polished off their sharp edges. I'd sealed what I could away in those damned jars and moved on into adulthood.

But maybe I'd gone too far. Had I stuffed the best part of my childhood in one of them and then planted a new life over it?

Why did I have to put an entire continent between me and my past? And why had I chosen to be so alone?

Did I suffer from mental illness like Mama had or something else?

I needed answers.

Annie Maude had always said that a few coincidences were just that. "But when they begin to gather like crows," she'd said, "you'd better pay attention, because unseen forces are at play."

Mama had believed in crows with ill intentions. She'd never felt safe in the world and had hidden her fragilities behind pills and lipstick. Whatever the truth: madness, evil spirits. or something I hadn't imagined. I wouldn't have wished any of those things on anybody.

In the kitchen, where I'd never cooked a meal for anyone, I set my coffee cup down. I moved into the living room, where no one had ever spilled wine on my floor, and I sat on the couch where nobody else had ever made themselves comfortable.

Nope. Nobody.

And in that moment, I needed someone like never before.

Yet I had no one to call, because all I had in the desert were acquaintances who'd had drinks with a carefully constructed version of myself. I hadn't let a single soul in. I'd given nothing.

The weight of that pressed down on me. I slid off onto the floor, hugged my knees, and hung my head. All that pent-up grief spilled out with the tears, with the drool and snot. I wailed and blubbered. I let go of dignity, vanity, rebellion. Most of all, I let go of the anger. That one had kept me spinning like a top, always one turn ahead of myself. Though inside I continued to be the little girl who would rather endure the taste of a copper penny in her mouth than cry, I'd grown up and my lucky penny had gone missing long ago.

I curled up on the floor, and cried myself out, until nothing remained but me. Just, Lucy.

Then, with the clarity that exhaustion sometimes brings, I thought of an answer, and I sat up.

I went to the storage closet where I'd put boxes of things I'd kept from my father's house. The puppet had been in one with photos. I pulled out the shoebox, threw off the lid, and clawed through the junk inside, hoping for any connection to home. Just pictures: Piano recital—*no*—tossed aside. Birthdays, Welcome to Virginia, my sister's ugly prom dress, uglier boyfriend—toss. Church picnics, more recitals.

Finally, I found something that struck a chord: A black and white photo with a scalloped border. Annie Maude and me, in her flower garden. She wore her apron, I sported a little straw hat, and we stood, fixed as history, with the sun illuminating our faces and secrets buried under our feet.

Yes, secrets....

...Under our feet, in the dirt...

I'd hidden my secrets from myself...

...In the jars...and then later inside my little red cabinet!

How could something I understood so well have become unbelievable?

In that moment, despite my years-long denial of the truth of Annie Maude's magic, I knew with a certainty that inside that cabinet I'd have my answers. Her methods were no idealistic notion, but a reality I had known.

Where would it be, the cabinet?

Realizing I'd foolishly lost track of something so important, my need to think otherwise bordered on panic. I grabbed onto the hope that Helen had kept the cabinet. She's sentimental that way, I told myself.

I went to the kitchen and splashed chilly water on my face, then patted my eyes and cheeks with a towel while I felt around in my purse. My phone contained my sister's number.

~ ~ ~

The crate arrived a week later, and I'd made quick work of opening it with my clawhammer.

Over the phone Helen had told me, "The day we sorted Daddy's house, I'd just returned from taking you to the airport, when Ruth arrived. Oh my God, how she had aged."

I could picture the scene as she spoke. Mr. Johnson's old truck had rattled up the driveway and Ruth stepped out. "Sharp-eyed and insistent, though frail," Helen had described her.

"She took me to the shed," Helen said, "pointed at the cabinet and told me to hold onto it for you, to keep it safe and closed. I thought to call you about it, but Ruth told me not to. She's one creepy old lady. I would've done anything she asked. I put it in my basement, figuring if you didn't ever ask for it, I might refinish it. It's kind of cute. Ruth promised me that one day you'd come back for it, and that when you did, you would come back to us."

She'd agreed to ship the cabinet.

I wrestled it out of the crate. Now the cabinet sat in the middle of my living room at the center of what looked like a blast radius of packing material. I approached reluctantly and opened the little doors that had been tied shut by their knobs. Helen had left the jars inside and stuffed the spaces between tightly with a mix of wadded paper and Styrofoam peanuts. I looked at the jar in front, and could see through the clouded glass a red ticket like those at the carnival.

~ ~ ~

No one stood in line for The Monster House. The operator, a bored-looking teen in a dirty white tee shirt waved my ticket away and gestured to the waiting car. Folding the ticket and putting it in my pocket, I sat and allowed him to click the safety bar into place. Having The Monster House all to myself suited me fine. I didn't get on the ride for fun—I did it for the shadows and the jerky motion of the cars, the movement and the numbing distraction. Although I wanted to forget about Bendyman, for some reason, I liked his ticket in my pocket. I pictured it on the mantel in my room, with my hair braid and other mementos. As the car lurched forward, I turned back to glimpse Daddy, who looked content with his cigarette, watching people pass by. I brushed off a bit of sawdust clinging to one of my knees. The car took me into the dark and noisy interior. The rocking of the car set up a rhythm, and I put words to it:

I lean to the left

…and a witch in black light poster colors shot out of the darkness to my right, coming dangerously close. She screamed, while calliope music, peppered with wild laughter, echoed along the corridor.

I lean to the right

…loud drumming stopped, and a hanged man dropped from above, his feet dangling inches from my head. I ducked though there was plenty of room.

I am a chalk line,

…flashes of light popped and snapped too close, a coffin lid opened with a shrieking creak, and a jerking, bloody corpse appeared.

A neon sign…

I closed my eyes for the rest of the ride, wanting just the jerky motion and the sounds.

Once the car slowed and curved around to stop at the beginning, I opened my eyes. Blinking in the lights, I saw Daddy where I'd left him, but now in conversation with another man.

The operator drew a circle in the air, then blew out a thick plume of smoke. "Wanna go again?" he asked. I nodded my head in answer, wondering if he felt sorry for me, a skinny kid on that lame ride, all alone. I closed my eyes again. The thought occurred to me that I might never ride The Monster House again—getting too old.

Again, I settled into the rocking of the car and put words to the rhythm.

> *And the tick and tock*
> *Of a run-down clock*
> *And down and down*
> *we go around*
> *we don't know which or whether,*

"We brought us here together!"
My eyes flew open—had I said that aloud?
A cold spot I didn't go through the last time around.
In the strobing light, I caught a glimpse of my hands, like pale spiders, clutching the bar.

Following a longer pause of darkness between flashes, four hands clutched the bar.

Someone rode beside me!

"*We* brought us here, *together*," came a voice in my ear, clear as a bell.

My scream became lost in the noise of the ride.

I couldn't get out of the car—the bar fit too low and snug over my legs. Leaning away from her, I turned to get a better look. She was me if I were dead. And now she sat where I had, and I beside her.

"Scare-a-boo, *got* you," she whispered and then gave me a grin full of rotten baby teeth.

I'd gone mad, like Mama!

I shrank from the dead presence beside me in The Monster House, and sat quaking painfully against the sheet-metal side of the car.

"Don't turn away," she said "I have to tell you something."

She leaned closer, her breath like one of those fetid tide pools on Edisto Island.

"Daddy knows about the man with the hat and Mama. He's going to get her back."

As I crouched on the floor of my apartment in the desert, the remembered words reached deep inside me and twisted like a key forcing a frozen lock.

My crying on the ride home in the car suddenly made sense: I was afraid for Daddy. I should have said something, warned him not to go after the man in the black fedora. I wanted to tell him there was nothing he could do, that he could not win against such a monster. I wanted to cry out, "Mama made her choice. I don't want to lose you too."

But how could I? How to tell him? I choked on my sobs and the words wouldn't come.

bone-weary, I told myself the ghost girl had lied. Why would I put stock in her words? She couldn't be real.

Exhaustion, grief, and too many candy apples—those were real.

At home, I went straight to bed.

In the morning, in full daylight, none of it seemed possible, the ghost girl, the idea that Daddy would have any way to find Mama, let alone the man in the black fedora.

Daddy's death the following week, in the same waters that had taken Mama, told me I'd been a fool not to believe, and that I'd failed him.

~ ~ ~

The jar lay on its side on the floor, the lid to one side. My hand had closed into a fist around the ticket. The red paper felt fairly alive against my palm.

I had to have a drink. Sitting at the kitchen table, holding a glass of whiskey in shaking hands, I stared at the ticket.

The ghost in the memory had been something forgotten, no doubt put in a jar long ago with the help of the ticket. No telling what else from my past I had put away in those jars. Opening one had shown me the consequences of ignoring Grandma's advice. With the complacency of my teen years, and a desire to be rid of painful memories, especially my sense of blame for Daddy's death, I had failed to make my yearly visits with the contents of the cabinet. If I suffered now, well, *no wonder*—chunks of my past, including lessons learned, had gone missing.

Had Mama indeed been involved with the man in the black fedora, even before Penny was born? When Mama took her own life, had she left all of us for him?

The answers were all in my cabinet. Opening the jars one at a time, I put the pieces of my past together until I'd completed the puzzle. I knew the ghost girl as Penny again and I became reacquainted with Mr. Charlie, along with numerous other, now trivial memories.

I rose from the floor and went to the balcony off my bedroom, saw the last colors of daylight fleeing over the mountains to the West. I had not eaten all day and still had no hunger. With an unreasonable fear that I might again forget about how Daddy died, I placed the red ticket in my shirt pocket. At bedtime, I tucked it into one of the compartments within my purse. Not at all sure why, I felt like it belonged there.

I moved through the following days like a ghost, not truly present.

Still, the opening to my show loomed. I went through the motions of setting up a gallery exhibit I no longer cared about.

~ ~ ~

Speeding to get to the opening for the exhibit, I hated my art, the Big Horn Pavilion, and the art world in general. What had I been thinking? My art—none of it good enough—didn't stack up to other artists' work I'd seen at the gallery. And what was I doing all dressed up for an event that no one I cared about would attend? My skirt had bunched up under my ass in the car seat and I couldn't get comfortable. I'd probably be a wrinkled mess when I got out. I'd never felt right in a skirt. The makeup I'd put on felt like a plastic coating. I'd slap-dashed it on fast, so chances were, I looked like one of the clowns in my exhibit. I laughed at the thought. Good, if I stand still, no one will know any different. The dashboard clock told me I'd arrive twenty minutes late. Stuck behind Ma and Pa *Slowbobeans*, I drummed my fingers on the wheel and resisted cursing out my window.

My mind still reeled at what I'd learned by opening the jars in my cabinet. Gallery parking would be impossible by now. Ahead, the intersections had become blocked by tourists in town for the festival. Fuck it—I'd hoof it for the next few blocks. Even in high heels, the walk would be faster than looking for a closer spot. I pulled into a one-hour parking zone, knowing I'd probably get a citation.

Opening the door, I got a blast of the desert heat. If I hurried, as I intended, I'd be dripping with sweat upon arrival. I tried to take my time, but couldn't.

Moving too fast, I didn't see the old man until I struck him with my shoulder. He must have just stepped out of the alley. Down he went. Poor old guy, he looked too fragile to take a fall. He lay groaning on the ground, clutching his elbow.

"I'm so sorry," I said, reaching to offer help. That's when I saw the "7" tattooed on his neck. He took my hand, and his face turned to me.

Pretzel...the convict...

BENDYMAN...

Here, *now!*

No way that could be real.

Though nearly dropping him, I held on until he found his feet.

Annie Maude's words came to me, "When coincidences gather like crows..."

Thin and wiry, but much older. Much, much older. Rather broken.

"Are you hurt?" I asked.

A cluster of people walked by, one of them brushing past me.

"Don't matter much in the scheme of things," he said, still rubbing his elbow.

"I can't believe it's you." The words spilled out before I could stop them.

He looked at me curiously. "Do I know you, missy?"

We stepped closer to the building to get out of the footpath so people could walk by more easily.

"We met when I was little, twice, in South Carolina."

"Well, I'll be John Brown."

"You're Pretzel, aren't you? I saw you at the county fair?"

"Pretzel, huh? Well, used to be. Ha! Can't claim that now, but I do what I can. As a matter of fact, I'm trying to earn my dinner." He gestured to a cigar box inside the alley, sitting next to a half empty bottle of water. He looked at me expectantly.

I glanced down at the single dollar and the coins scattered in the box.

"How about I buy your dinner instead?"

He gave me a suspicious look like I tried to play him somehow. That's when I saw the ex-con again. Finally, he smiled, and instead of gold teeth, I saw yellowed dentures.

"That would be a fine thing, miss–?"

"Just Lucy."

"And I'm Nestor Lee Finechel."

We settled into a booth at the rear of one of those trendy California diners. The fixtures were vintage 1960's, which seemed right, under the circumstances. I ordered coffee and he got the blue plate special, with extra mashed potatoes.

"I've walked by this place plenty, but I've never been inside. Not bad." He craned his neck, looking around, startling the old ladies in the booth behind him. I couldn't tell if they'd reacted that way because his head had turned so far around on his neck or because of his rough appearance. One glared at me as if to say, "What are you doing with the likes of him."

Thoughts of the gallery returned. They'd be wondering where the hell I'd gone.

Somehow the show didn't matter anymore. Fuck 'em—they knew where to send the check. Annie Maude's advice told me that being with Pretzel was more important. Not heeding her hadn't worked out too well.

"You're a long way from South Carolina," he said. "What brings you here?"

"I ran away from home years ago. This seemed far enough that no one would bother me."

"Trouble?"

"Not with others. I was trying to get away from myself."

"How'd you do?"

"I followed me. Now I just try not to look in the mirror." My hollow laugh seemed to surprise him. He *has no idea*, I decided, then thought that maybe he did, after all. "What about you?"

I've been knockin' around carnivals all over for the better part of fifty years. Got sick—cancer—and stayed here for the warm weather. I sure do miss the seasons, though. Nothing beats a crisp fall day in South Carolina."

And for a moment, I returned to *my* October: The late, golden light, leaves blowing on a scented wind, the thrill of carnival, and finally the red ticket he gave me.

I took the ticket from my purse and placed it on the table between us.

Pretzel looked at it vacantly.

"You gave that to me when I was thirteen years old."

He lifted his eyes to mine, and a crease formed down the middle of his forehead. He looked down at the ticket again, and his face seemed to search for an expression. A bit of mashed potato that had clung to the corner of his mouth, fell off. He looked at me again, and his mouth worked but no sounds emerged. Tears gathered at the corners of his eyes, and he quickly wiped them away.

"I d-did?" he stammered; his voice full of emotion.

Had he become upset with me?

No, something else. I saw in his eyes the same sense of wonder I had at the confluence of events that had brought us together. They could not be mere coincidences.

"May I have the ticket?"

Without knowing why, I didn't want to give it up. Yet, somehow I couldn't say no.

He reached for it, hesitated, glancing at me.

"Yes," I said.

Nestor gulped a breath and began to weep silently. He buried his face in his hands and struggled to hold himself together.

I reached across and placed a hand on his arm. He lowered that hand, and I placed the ticket in his palm. Tears fell down my face, and I didn't know why.

"Are you alright?" I asked.

"I will be, now." He barked a laugh, said, "Thick-headed old fool that I am, I didn't believe him."

"Believe who?"

"The man in mourning clothes, he comes to me in the night, while I'm sleeping."

Gooseflesh crawled up my back and neck, and down my arms, along with an urge to get up and get out. I belonged at the gallery, a well-lit public space full of people with mundane lives and meaningless conversation.

But I stayed. I had to know.

"A caretaker? Are you in a shelter or care facility?"

"No, just a room in the flophouse. Different rooms, different times."

Then I knew for certain.

"He frightens you, doesn't he?"

"Not anymore. Not as much as the pain. She's a cruel companion in my bed each night, insists on cuddling too close. And him—come to find he doesn't mean any harm. He's just the way of things. I've been ready for some time, but when he asks for my ticket, I've had nothing to give him." He held up the red carnival ticket.

"Will that work?"

"Can't help but work. He told me to keep an eye out, that sooner or later the ticket would find me. And here *you* are, Lucy."

"Is there something more I can do, Nestor?"

"No, I've had a satisfying meal, thanks to you, and I'm headed home."

Home. Yes, that's where I should be.

"Me too," I said, and I almost thanked him for sending me back to South Carolina in October. Knowing he wouldn't understand, I said simply, "Thank you, Nestor."

Although I'd have to come back for my stuff, if I booked a flight that night, I'd get home in time for Halloween.

Home

I couldn't afford a house on the Savannah River, but found one not too far from Annie Maude's old house. When the van finally arrived with my stuff from the desert and the moving company men were unloading it, I made a pain in the ass of myself directing traffic.

With so much to do, the questions didn't frighten me anymore, and the few that remained—the mystery of Grandma's and Ruth's involvement with the man in the black fedora, whether he had been menacing me, and if Penny had been lying about Mama going off with him—had been whittle to fine, unanswerable points.

What Nestor had said of the man fit with my suspicions, but I have nothing more to add to that.

If Mama did go with that fellow, I liked to think Daddy had somehow won her back.

Most of my studio remained boxed up while I set up my workbench beside a window—the afternoon had shown me that the light would be good there.

Once the decision had been made to return to South Carolina, I knew what my first project would be: A picture book about a ghost-girl named Penny I planned to title *Miss Myrtle's Home for Little, Lost Ghosts*. Well past sunset, I arranged my writing supplies and a sketch pad in preparation for beginning the work, and sat.

I was too exhausted, though, after a day of trying furniture in different configurations and shifting boxes of my crap around. Family would have helped, yet I wanted to settle in before I let anyone know I'd returned.

The little black button eye I'd placed on my bench still held onto a tiny scrap of fabric. I picked the eye up and examined it closely. Bunny had required a lot of repairs over the years. Because Mama had a better way with needle and thread, at the time I didn't understand why Daddy insisted on being the one to fix Bunny. The last time the eye came off, he'd sewn it back on with ten-pound fishing line. "Let's see how *that* works," he said, then kissed my head and chuckled.

The line had held. The last time it came undone, the button had been torn off or perhaps *bitten* off. Again, I pictured those blackened baby teeth in Penny's ghostly head. Somehow, they weren't so scary anymore.

I knew now why Annie Maude had always cracked a window. My studio would be cold in the morning, but I opened the window and placed the button on the sill all the same. I closed the door behind me and headed for bed.

14
Clocks
(An excerpt from Miss Myrtle's Home for Little, Lost Ghosts by Lucy A. Moxley)

The house has a hundred clocks. Each ticks away the seconds and minutes according to its own mechanism, day and night. The result is a permanent, complex persistence of clicking, ticking and tocking. Since the clocks are slightly out of synch, their collective sound modulates continuously, slipping into temporary rhythms, like when windshield wipers match up with the radio's music, then fall apart as soon as you notice. Like figures in moving clouds, like glimpses of ghosts, or the shapes in the murmurings of blackbirds. They don't hold. The one constant is the *fact* of the ticking.

And there is the marking of the hours. Chimes, bells, and birds that always begin with a single note, grow swiftly to a cacophony that approaches the very doorstep of madness, finally diminishing and ending with a single, straggling tone. The hour has been served. The seconds reassert themselves with clicking, ticking and tocking, and the house resumes its breathing.

With such a dynamic, once in a blue moon, something happens: The various hourly chimes find a rare choreography that swells the hearts of any who hear it. Every creature in the house, down to the smallest of mice, and the meekest of ghosts, stops to listen together. This is the music of the endless. This is the music of joy that surpasses understanding. And it *holds*...long enough, and strong enough, to leave its mark on the memory of every spirit.

During one of these rarest of events, the front door opens, and Miss Myrtle enters, hand in hand with a little girl. The girl seems fragile. All dark hair and big eyes, she surveys the spacious interior spread out before her. As the chimes fade, the heartbeat of the house resumes, and she is enveloped in a warmth she's never known.

The girl's name is Penny, and though the idea isn't yet a thought, she is finally home.

End

Afterword

I've spent the afternoon stress-cleaning the kitchen. The news is all bad—the death toll from the pandemic rises daily, riots, politics that seem downright criminal, machinations against most of us. Damn it to Hell, I *will* control this one room. The weather has finally warmed enough to open windows. As my hands work in the soapy water, I watch sunlight play over dandelions scattered like stars across the yard outside. In my mind's eye, I see Bilbo rolling around out there, with that glow cats get when they're happy. Dogs are more obvious with their joy. They bound about, tongues flopping, ears flapping, tails wagging, and I love them for it. A cat's joy shines from within. Bilbo had been lit up most of his life. I sure miss that big old cat.

I'm home alone today, with the music turned up, and the squirrels lively and loud in a nearby tree. I put the last of the plates away and wipe the counter around a neat tray of ingredients gathered for baking chocolate chip cookies. My thoughts snap to Phillip.

He was my first-born. I'd been twenty-four, with lofty ideas, and little common sense.

My mother had been ill, and died within a month of his arrival. A year later, his father and I split up. I'd been the one to leave.

I took few possessions, mostly clothes, the baby's things, and Phillip. At the time, I thought I'd done my best. I may have been wrong about that. I still question myself in the worst and most punishing ways. *What if? Why didn't I?* I wonder how Phillip's life might have been different if I'd made more measured choices, been less of a mess.

He joined the army after high school. I followed his journey in the letters he sent. They were nearly always two sheets, filled front and back with his small, neat printing, except when he added poetry. The poems appeared in long, narrow strips, surrounded by ample space, fragile bridges over water. The training and Korean culture broadened his perspective, as evidenced by his words. In his third year of service there, his unit went to quell a riot. A concrete block, thrown from stories up, struck his helmet. He was hospitalized in Seoul, then flown back to Georgia. Just like that, at twenty-three, he'd become a veteran. The blow took the peripheral vision in one eye and left him with recurring mini-strokes and occasional horrific and crippling hallucinations in which he feared what he might turn into. Still, he'd managed to finish college, take a counselor position at the VA, fall in love, and marry. He tried an ever-changing assortment of prescriptions and therapies, he self-medicated with caffeine, alcohol, and pot, the combined results unreliable and sometimes destructive. He collected AA chips in a dresser drawer. His own failures and victories made him compassionate and astute. He became a dedicated and talented advocate for other veterans. He'd always been a goofball, a gifted poet, and a card-carrying nerd—an active member of The Society for Creative Anachronism. He loved his wife, and their friends loved him. At the funeral, they told colorful stories.

Phillip had never been what you'd call normal. He had never been *safe,* even in childhood. By the time he turned fifteen, he'd started at least three fires. One of them had needed the fire department. His sisters have endless stories.

I last saw him in November, three years ago. My children had all traveled from their homes in different parts of the country to visit: Aubrey, Alison and her son, Logan, Phillip and his wife, Melissa. David (Aubrey's dad) had also come. A good week-long reunion. Our house filled with their voices and laughter.

They wanted to see a dispensary. Oregon had been one of the first states to legalize pot, and Eugene's dispensaries had achieved the status of tourist attractions. We went as a group, with Phillip squeezed into the way-back of the Element. Halfway home, he'd started giggling.

"Did you get into the edibles already?" Aubrey asked him.

He popped his head up from behind the seats, said, "I love chocolate chips…" and disappeared again.

"Exactly how much of that pot cookie did you eat?" she asked

"Both of them!" he said.

"Predictably, Phillip the extreme," David said.

Two months later, on an evening in January, as usual, he arrived home from work and kissed Melissa in their kitchen on the way to shower and change. But instead, at some point, while she made dinner, he locked the door, took his gun from the closet and ended his life.

Phillip…*gone.*

Irrevocably, life as I'd come to know it ended. I hadn't spoken with him that day. I'd sent him a picture of a squirrel—the sort of *normal* thing we did.

The day had been a normal one in my house: Orion had a swim meet, and there had been talk of snow. A normal, unremarkable day right up until the phone call that shattered me and the rest of our family.

The next day, I awoke to a reality in which one of my sons had stepped away forever.

That had also been the day Trump was sworn into office.

For me, events large and small have the potential to become hard, solid, dividing lines. The universe is broken into two parts: the *before* and the *after*. With momentous events—September 11th, 2001, November 4th, 2016, January 6th, 2021, along with births, deaths, first kisses, and lost jobs—lines appear. This pandemic will likely be a broad stroke. I fear to think of the line that might come next.

People can get divided too, on the inside. This was true for me. Before that terrible January day, I'd been one person, afterward, someone else. I cannot overstate this. Sometimes, I can tell that others don't see that I'm no longer who they think I am, and that can lead to me feeling like an imposter. I don't get out much, and I don't dance.

That's who I am on this particular day in April when, in the middle of my therapy housework, I connect to the memory of chocolate chips and Phillip. The gut-punch jolts me. The world goes crooked for a moment and the tears come. But this time, I stay on my feet. I take several deep breaths, drink some water, and step outside with glass for the recycling. Reaching the bin, I spot my neighbor across the fence. He's watering his roses. He has a joyous expression, he's lit by the sun, and he's glory-to-God-butt-ass naked. Before I can gather myself and dart back inside, he turns to face me, and we make eye contact.

Oh no!

He waves at me and grins; a child's grin, a child's wave. That, despite his thick, dark beard, and all that goes with that. His open, innocent expression is as unexpected as his nudity, so much so that I simply smile back sheepishly, and lift my own hand.

This, then, is another sort of jolt. A reminder that pain, however deep, is merely one part of my story.

I can *never* know what the next moment will bring.

I go back inside and chuckle quietly, shaking my head, while my eyes are still wet from crying. On the playlist, "Helplessly Hoping" has given way to "Diamond Girl."

Phillip would have liked this new neighbor. Probably. He always said that normal people might be safe, but he didn't find them interesting.

I know, Monkey. You are my son.

The conquered kitchen seems sterile. The room wants the smell of baking cookies and maybe a little spilled flour; something to welcome my other son and my husband home. I take out the heavy mixing bowl that once belonged to my grandmother, and Mama's hand-written recipe book.

—Lisa Snellings
Eugene Oregon

Lisa Snellings grew up in South Carolina, where her favorite pastimes were reading science fiction and horror books and making art with any medium available. Her unique artistic perspective was further informed by her first job at a hospital, specifically in its basement morgue. A fascination for county fairs and her family's deep involvement in religion added to the mix, resulting in beautiful, whimsical, and sometimes macabre sculptures. These found captive audiences at speculative fiction conventions, drawing the attention of authors she had grown up reading. Her kinetic carnival collection, "Dark Caravan," premiered at the 59th World Science Fiction Convention in 2001 and eventually made its way to the American Visionary Art Museum in 2010. The artist has enjoyed collaborating with the likes of Neil Gaiman, Harlan Ellison, Larry Niven and Peter S. Beagle. Her "Poppets," two-inch-tall figurines that mimic "silly humans," are collected around the world. www.patreon.com/lisasnellings

After nearly two decades in the Southern California desert, Lisa lives in Eugene, Oregon with her husband, Pete Clark, son, Orion Clark, and two ever-present cats.

Author, illustrator, and publisher, Alan M. Clark, grew up in Tennessee in a house full of bones and old medical books. In his thirty-seven years as a freelance illustrator, he has created illustrations for hundreds of books, including works of fiction of various genres, nonfiction, textbooks, young adult fiction, and children's books. During his twenty-seven years as a freelance writer, he has authored twenty-two published books, including fifteen novels, a lavishly illustrated novella, a lavishly illustrated novellette, four collections of fiction, and a nonfiction full-color book of his artwork. Honors for his work include the World Fantasy Award, four Chesley Awards, and he is an International Book Awards winner. Alan M. Clark and his wife, Melody, live in Oregon. www.alanmclark.com

IFD Publishing Paperbacks

Novels:
Of Thimble and Threat, by Alan M. Clark
Baggage Check, by Elizabeth Engstrom
Bull's Labyrinth, by Eric Witchey
The Surgeon's Mate: A Dismemoir, by Alan M. Clark
Siren Promised, by Jeremy Robert Johnson and Alan M. Clark
Say Anything but Your Prayers, by Alan M. Clark
Candyland, by Elizabeth Engstrom
Apologies to the Cat's Meat Man, by Alan M. Clark
Lizzie Borden, by Elizabeth Engstrom
A Parliament of Crows, by Alan M. Clark
Lizard Wine, by Elizabeth Engstrom
The Door that Faced West, by Alan M. Clark
The Northwoods Chronicles, by Elizabeth Engstrom
The Prostitute's Price, by Alan M. Clark
The Assassin's Coin, by John Linwood Grant
13 Miller's Court, by Alan M. Clark and John Linwood Grant
Guys Named Bob, by Elizabeth Engstrom
Fallen Giants of the Points, by Alan M. Clark
The Itinerant, by Elizabeth Engstrom
York's Moon, by Elizabeth Engstrom
Night Birds, by Lisa Snellings and Alan M. Clark

Collections:
Professor Witchey's Miracle Mood Cure, by Eric Witchey

Nonfiction:
How to Write a Sizzling Sex Scene, by Elizabeth Engstrom
Divorce by Grand Canyon, by Elizabeth Engstrom

IFD Publishing EBooks

(You can find the following titles at most distribution points for all ereading platforms.)

Novels:
The Prostitute's Price, by Alan M. Clark
The Assassin's Coin, by John Linwood Grant
13 Miller's Court, by Alan M. Clark and John Linwood Grant
Guys Named Bob, by Elizabeth Engstrom

Apologies to the Cat's Meat Man, by Alan M. Clark
Bull's Labyrinth, by Eric Witchey
The Surgeon's Mate: A Dismemoir, by Alan M. Clark
York's Moon, by Elizabeth Engstrom
Beyond the Serpent's Heart, by Eric Witchey
Lizzie Borden, by Elizabeth Engstrom
A Parliament of Crows, by Alan M. Clark
Lizard Wine, by Elizabeth Engstrom
Northwoods Chronicles, by Elizabeth Engstrom
Siren Promised, by Alan M. Clark and Jeremy Robert Johnson
To Kill a Common Loon, by Mitch Luckett
The Man in the Loon, by Mitch Luckett
Of Thimble and Threat by Alan M. Clark
Jack the Ripper Victim Series: The Double Event (includes two novels from the series: *Of Thimble and Threat* and *Say Anything But Your Prayers*) by Alan M. Clark
Candyland, by Elizabeth Engstrom
The Blood of Father Time: Book 1, The New Cut, by Alan M. Clark, Stephen C. Merritt & Lorelei Shannon
The Blood of Father Time: Book 2, The Mystic Clan's Grand Plot, by Alan M. Clark, Stephen C. Merritt & Lorelei Shannon
How I Met My Alien Bitch Lover: Book 1 from the Sunny World Inquisition Daily Letter Archives, by Eric Witchey
Baggage Check, by Elizabeth Engstrom
D. D. Murphry, Secret Policeman, by Alan M. Clark and Elizabeth Massie
Black Leather, by Elizabeth Engstrom
Fallen Giants of the Points, by Alan M. Clark
The Itinerant, by Elizabeth Engstrom
Night Birds, by Lisa Snellings and Alan M. Clark

Novelettes:
Mudlarks and the Silent Highwayman, by Alan M. Clark
The Tao of Flynn, by Eric Witchey
To Build a Boat, Listen to Trees, by Eric Witchey

Children's Illustrated:
The Christmas Thingy, by F. Paul Wilson. Illustrated by Alan M. Clark

Collections:
Suspicions, by Elizabeth Engstrom
Professor Witchey's Miracle Mood Cure, by Eric Witchey

Short Fiction:
"Brittle Bones and Old Rope," by Alan M. Clark

"Crosley," by Elizabeth Engstrom
"The Apple Sniper," by Eric Witchey

Nonfiction:

How to Write a Sizzling Sex Scene, by Elizabeth Engstrom
Divorce by Grand Canyon, by Elizabeth Engstrom

IFD Publishing Audio Books

Novels:

The Door That Faced West by Alan M. Clark, read by Charles Hinckley
Jack the Ripper Victim Series: Of Thimble and Threat, by Alan M. Clark, read by Alicia Rose
Jack the Ripper Victim Series: Say Anything But Your Prayers, by Alan M. Clark, read by Alicia Rose
Jack the Ripper Victim Series: The Double Event by Alan M. Clark, read by Alicia Rose (includes two novels from the series: *Of Thimble and Threat* and *Say Anything But Your Prayers*)
A Parliament of Crows by Alan M. Clark, read by Laura Jennings
A Brutal Chill in August by Alan M. Clark, read by Alicia Rose
The Surgeon's Mate: A Dismemoir, by Alan M. Clark, read by Alan M. Clark
Apologies to the Cat's Meat Man, by Alan M. Clark, read by Alicia Rose
The Prostitute's Price, by Alan M. Clark, read by Alicia Rose
The Assassin's Coin, by John Linwood Grant, read by Alicia Rose
13 Miller's Court, by Alan M. Clark and John Linwood Grant, read by Alicia Rose

Novelettes:

Mudlarks and the Silent Highwayman, by Alan M. Clark, read by Alicia Rose

CPSIA information can be obtained
at www.ICGtesting.com
Printed in the USA
LVHW100706170622
721513LV00004B/362

9 798985 282733